"Ma, can I ask you something?"

"You know you can."

Adam nodded. "I was just wondering." His young brow furrowed as he considered his next words. "Would you be angry with me if I, um, if I went to work for Mr. O'Keefe?"

"Are you sure?"

"Yes, Ma, because he was right, you know."

"About what?"

"About not being able to get any sleep, on account of I'd feel bad about what I did. I don't like feeling guilty. I have a conscience, Ma, I do!"

"Of course you have a conscience. Whatever made you think you didn't?"

He leaned a cheek on a doubled-up fist. "Well," he began, poking his fork tine into the skin of his fried egg, "I just did things before, you know, without thinking about what other folks might think—if it made 'em angry, or hurt their feelings, or. . ."

"You've been thinking about all that, just because of what Mr. O'Keefe said?"

Adam nodded. "Uh-huh." He sat up straight. "So can I, Ma? Can I work at the warehouse, to pay for the lunches I stole?"

She took a sip of her coffee, more to forestall the tears than to figure out what she'd tell her son. *He's growing up,* she admitted, he's becoming a man, *thanks to John Joseph O'Keefe!*

.

LOREE LOUGH has written twenty-two inspirational novels for adults and children and more than 2,000 articles and dozens of short stories. Loree teaches writing and, even off-duty, loves talking about it. Loree lives in Maryland with her husband, daughters, and two constantly warring cats.

HEARTSONG PRESENTS
Books by Loree Lough
HP86—Pocketful of Love
HP151—Follow the Leader
HP157—Pocketful of Promises
HP161—Montana Sky
HP167—Priscilla Hires a Husband
HP227—Bridget's Bargain
HP232—Emma's Orphans

Books under the pen name Cara McCormack
HP147—Drewry's Bluff
HP175—James' Joy

Don't miss out on any of our super romances. Write to us at the following address for information on our newest releases and club information.

Heartsong Presents Readers' Service
P.O. Box 719
Uhrichsville, OH 44683

Kate Ties
The Knot

Loree Lough

Heartsong Presents

To Carolyn Males, the first published author to say, "You can do it, Loree!" and to all the other writers—multi-published and pre-published—whose participation in writers' critique groups helped me believe it.

A note from the author:
I love to hear from my readers! You may write to me at the following address: **Loree Lough**
Author Relations
P.O. Box 719
Uhrichsville, OH 44683

ISBN 1-57748-252-2

KATE TIES THE KNOT

© 1997 by Barbour Publishing, Inc. All rights reserved. Except for use in any review, the reproduction or utilization of this work in whole or in part in any form by any electronic, mechanical, or other means, now known or hereafter invented, is forbidden without the permission of the publisher, Heartsong Presents, P.O. Box 719, Uhrichsville, Ohio 44683.

All of the characters and events in this book are fictitious. Any resemblance to actual persons, living or dead, or to actual events is purely coincidental.

Cover illustration by Chris Cocozza.

PRINTED IN THE U.S.A.

one

Currituck, North Carolina
1855

The huge, hollering loud Irishman had been hot on the boy's heels for half a mile. Eight-year-old Adam Flynn raced into his mother's shop for protection, nearly overturning a dressmaker's dummy as he rounded the corner.

"What's gotten into you, son?" his mother demanded. "Haven't I taught you better than to—"

"So there ye are, ye thievin' little brat!"

The burly, bearded man who filled the doorway reminded Adam of Jack's Giant, fists clenched at his sides, feet planted shoulder width apart. Adam had heard dozens of stories about J. J. O'Keefe, among them, that he'd literally fought for the money to erect his shipbuilding warehouse. The boy sidled closer to his mother. "Hand over me lunch," O'Keefe growled, extending a meaty palm, "before I hand ye over to the constable."

His mother stood and put a protective arm around her boy's shoulders. "I don't know who you think you are," she huffed, "barging in here, frightening my boy, but I won't tolerate such behavior in my shop."

He matched her angry gaze. "Who I am, ma'am, is John Joseph O'Keefe." His expression and his voice softened to add, "I apologize for stampeding in here—"

"Like a raging bull?" she interrupted.

Grinning sheepishly, he answered, "Well, I wasn't goin' to put it quite that strongly, but 'rampagin' bull' will do, I guess."

For a moment, the adults merely stood toe to toe, arms

crossed, chins lifted in stubborn determination, like odd-sized, eerie reflections of one another. Adam stared gap-jawed, wondering who would break the silence, his tiny mother, or this tall, intimidating man.

"I know who you are," she said, breaking the silence. "You may have every man in town intimidated, but you don't scare me!"

When a corner of O'Keefe's mustachioed mouth lifted in a wry grin, Adam relaxed.

Too soon. O'Keefe turned to Adam. "Ye ought to be ashamed of yerself, hidin' behind yer ma's skirts. Are ye a coward as well as a thief?"

"How dare you! My boy never stole anything in his life."

O'Keefe never took his eyes off Adam as he lifted his brown-bearded chin. Lifted an eyebrow, too. "Then maybe ye'd care to explain what he's got tucked under his arm, there," came the gravelly suggestion. " 'Tisn't a fat red hen," he added, pointing. "I can tell ye that."

She followed his gaze to the lunch bucket under Adam's arm. "What—? Where—? How did you get this?" she demanded, taking it from him.

He looked from his mother's anxious face to O'Keefe's—which was strangely calm now—and back again. Placing a hand on her forearm, he whimpered deliberately, "I didn't know it was his, Ma."

O'Keefe expelled a puff of air, reminding Adam now of a fire-breathing dragon. "I feel sorry for yer ma," he fumed, "havin' a thief, a coward, and a liar for a son." His gray eyes narrowed. "Ye know as well as I do that ye stole me lunch today, just like ye stole it yesterday, and the day before." The first two fingers of his right hand straddled his nose, rested on his cheekbones. "I saw ye, with me own two eyes. Practice behavin' like a man, why don't ye, and own up to yer dirty deed?"

He'd never been afraid for his life before, but Adam had

been plenty scared minutes ago when O'Keefe's big booted feet thundered closer, harder, behind him. But he was safe now, in the shelter of his mother's arms, and he knew it. Adam aimed a cocksure smirk at the man, fully prepared to continue professing his innocence. What choice did he have? If he admitted his guilt, his ma would punish him by adding all sorts of miserable chores to his already too-long list.

From the corner of his eye, he noticed his mother was looking at him with a sideways, suspicious sort of look. He'd never seen anything like it on her face before. Was she angry? Sad? Hurt? Well, his ma wasn't one to dwell on his shortcomings, especially if teary eyes and a quivering lip were part of his apology. He held his breath, and began working on it.

"Well, don't just stand there, snifflin' like a girl, lad. 'Fess up!"

The production of tears was forgotten as Adam stiffened his back. "I'm not a girl!" he insisted, grabbing the bucket from his mother. "Here, take your stupid old lunch pail, if it means that much to you!" Without getting too far from his mother's side, he thrust it into O'Keefe's waiting hands. "It's probably full of worms anyway."

His mother pressed a palm to each blushing cheek and closed her eyes. Adam rolled his eyes. He knew what that meant: She was saying a silent prayer for strength. One fleeting second passed before she opened her eyes. "Oh, Adam," she whispered, her voice trembling slightly, "what have you done?"

He'd have given anything not to have put that pained, disappointed look on her face. If O'Keefe hadn't been standing there, frowning and shaking his head, Adam might have wrapped his arms around his mother, told her how much he loved her, how sorry he was to have hurt her. He'd have apologized for taking something that wasn't his and admitted he knew better than that.

But the man had called him a girl, and Bobby and the other

boys who'd been with him when he ran off with the lunch were hovering around the door. They'd hear everything.

Standing taller, Adam shrugged and made a face that told them all that a dented-up old lunch bucket wasn't worth all this fuss and bother.

His mother folded her hands in front of her. "I can assure you, Mr. O'Keefe, that nothing like this will ever happen again."

During the long silence that followed her promise, Adam watched O'Keefe carefully. A minute ago, he looked as if he wanted to take me over his knee. *Now he looks like he wants to hug Ma. Those stories about him are true, he told himself, Mr. O'Keefe is crazy!*

As if to prove it, the man aimed his glaring, gray gaze at Adam. "Say ye're sorry, why don't ye, so we can put this thing behind us?" He hesitated, and when Adam remained silent, added, "Don't tell me ye're waitin' for yer ma to do it for ye!"

Adam made a thin line of his mouth and folded both arms over his chest. Those boys would see Adam Flynn was no girl!

O'Keefe combed long, stubby fingers through his beard. "So we can add 'stubborn' to yer list o' faults," he said, shaking his head. "All right, then."

He bent forward slightly, and resting both hands on his knees, put himself eye-level with the boy. "Yer name is Adam, is it?"

Brow furrowed, the boy said nothing.

"How old are ye, Adam?"

"Eight." For the benefit of the older youngsters peering in the window, he added, "And three quarters."

O'Keefe nodded. "Well, Adam Eight-and-Three-Quarters, ye owe me for three lunches and the buckets they was packed in." Holding out one big palm, he rubbed his four fingertips against his thumb.

The youngster had seen the gesture enough times to know it

meant the man expected money. And he'd heard enough of O'Keefe's handiwork in the ring to know he'd better at least try to make good on his debt. Suddenly, his mother's protection seemed woefully inadequate. As he struggled for a comeback that might appease the ex-boxer, she stepped behind the counter, unlocked her cash box, and withdrew a silver dollar. Marching purposefully up to O'Keefe, she dropped it into his upturned palm. "I'm sure that will more than cover your losses."

Was she out of her mind? The old lunch bucket wasn't worth a whole dollar. Why, it probably wasn't worth a dime. Besides, it was the last dollar they had 'til old man Howard paid her for the dress she was making for his daughter.

O'Keefe merely stood, looking back and forth from the coin to his mother's face. Was he daft? Hadn't he ever seen a silver dollar before? " 'Twasn't you who stole me lunches," he said softly, wrapping his thick fingers around her slender wrist. "Shouldn't be you who pays for 'em." He pressed the dollar into her hand, took a step back and focused on Adam again. Crossing both arms over his barrel chest, he said, "Don't tell me ye're just goin' to stand there and let yer ma fight yer battles for ye?"

Squirming under the intense scrutiny of penetrating gray eyes, Adam focused on the floor. In the past, folks never paid much attention to his fatherless status. During the last few weeks, however, having no pa had helped him get away with all sorts of mischief. Why wasn't it working on O'Keefe? Flustered and afraid, he said, "But, mister, I don't have any money. Besides, it wasn't my idea. I wasn't the only one who—"

"Ye're the one that ran off with the lunches," O'Keefe pointed out. "And ye'll work at me warehouse 'til I say we're square."

Eyes wide as hen's eggs, Adam's mouth dropped open. "Me? Work in your—"

"Mr. O'Keefe," his mother interrupted, "I realize you haven't been in town very long, so perhaps you're not aware that my boy doesn't have a father." She nodded at the coin, winking up from where he'd put it in her hand. "Won't you let me reimburse—?"

"I'm not so new that I don't know who ye are," he said flatly. "Ye're Kate Flynn, widow o' one Sean Flynn." His gravelly voice softened considerably when he said, "I'm sorry for yer loss, ma'am, truly I am."

He shot a stern glance at Adam. "But not havin' a da is no excuse for stealin'. What the boy done was wrong."

Eyes and tone gentle again, he concluded, "It's up to him to make it right."

For a full minute, it seemed, no one moved, no one spoke. O'Keefe's gravelly baritone cracked the quiet. "Tell ye what, lad," he said, heading for the exit, "I'll leave it up to you. Pay the debt, or don't." He shrugged. "Won't be me who'll see the Dark Fairy in me dreams if ye don't make things right."

The Dark Fairy? Adam had no idea who or what the Dark Fairy might be. He only knew from O'Keefe's tone that it was someone—or something—to be reckoned with. He shivered involuntarily as O'Keefe turned to leave.

The man paused in the open door. "But let me leave ye wi' this to think on. If ye've even a pinstripe of good left in ye after rubbin' elbows with those ruffians, havin' this debt hangin' over yer head'll nag at ye like an aged fishwife. When ye're ready to ease yer conscience, ye know where to find me."

Conscience? Adam had been hearing the word for as long as he could remember. He wasn't sure, exactly, what a conscience was. Something you grew into, he presumed, like those other words adults bandied about: responsibility, sensibility, discernment. He'd obviously not grown up enough to have developed a conscience yet, because if he had, wouldn't it have "nagged" at him about something by now?

Sunshine, glinting in through the window, gleamed from the silver dollar his mother placed on the counter. *O'Keefe must have a pinstripe of good in him, too, because at least he's not taking our grocery money,* Adam thought, breathing a sigh of relief.

His mother clasped both hands at her waist and plastered her politest "for-customers-only" smile on her face. "Good day, Mr. O'Keefe," she said.

She could be painfully to-the-point when she wanted to be. And judging by O'Keefe's surprised reaction, she'd made her point.

"G'day to you, Mrs. Flynn."

And just like that, he was gone. Ordinarily, when adults chastised him for childhood pranks, feelings of resentment and anger sizzled inside Adam. O'Keefe had been far tougher on him than any grown-up to date, so it surprised him, as he watched the man cross the street and head back to his workshop, that he felt nothing of the kind.

What he felt instead was an uneasy, stinging sensation, prickling in his belly and poking at his brain.

A sign that he was developing a conscience?

🙚

"I understand you had company earlier."

Kate looked up from her sewing. "I imagine everyone within a two-mile radius knows I had a visitor this afternoon," she told her elderly neighbor. "Even he admitted he behaved like a 'rampaging bull'!"

Thaddius Crofton pulled up a chair and helped himself to a cookie. "Way I hear it, Adam had it comin'. He's been making a pest of himself all over town the last couple of weeks," he said around a mouthful of oatmeal raisin. "What's eatin' at the boy?"

She shrugged and met his pale blue eyes. "I'm not sure. Maybe it's those boys he's been hanging around with, putting ideas in his head." Sighing, Kate added, "I don't know what

I'm going to do with him."

"You're gonna let him work off his debt, that's what." The elderly gent took another bite of the cookie. "Little hard work never hurt anybody, least of all a boy who thinks he's entitled to help himself to what ain't his."

"He's only eight. He can't do a man's work."

"J. J.'s a decent fellow. I'm sure he won't give the boy more than he can handle."

"But that warehouse is no doubt filled with all sorts of dangerous tools. He might get hurt."

Chuckling, Thaddius pointed an arthritic finger at her sewing table, where scissors and razors, needles and pins lay in an orderly row. "He's managed to stay safe enough around the tools of your trade. Besides, eight is old enough to have some good old-fashioned horse sense."

She bit her lower lip. "I suppose you're right."

Thaddius reached across the space that separated them and gave her hand an affectionate pat. " 'Course I'm right. I'm always right. Just ask Mary." Then, with a merry wink, he said, "Aw, now don't look so worried, Kate. 'Train up a child in the way he should go, and when he is old he will not depart from it.'" He smiled. "You're a good woman. Strongest I've ever met. Good mother, too. You'll do what's right. You always have."

Setting her sewing aside, Kate stood. "Thanks, Thaddius," she said, handing him another cookie. "Now get on back to your own store before Mary puts the sheriff on your trail."

"You're the one ought to be afraid of the little woman," he teased, tipping the treat like a high silk hat. "That wife of mine don't take well to folks spoiling my supper, y'know."

The tiny bell above the door tinkled quietly when it closed behind him. Kate focused on her work, hoping it would help distract her from the worries that had been nagging at her lately.

It had all started several weeks ago, one evening just after supper. Adam had shoved his plate aside and propped both elbows on the table. "What really happened to my father?" he'd asked, elfin chin propped on his fists.

She'd looked into his trusting blue eyes and wondered how much truth he could handle. Kate had seldom lied to her only child, and even then, only the lie of omission. Shouldn't she protect him for at least a little while longer?

"You already know what happened, Adam. Your father was. . ." Even after seven years, she found it next to impossible to say. "He was shot."

"I know, I know, by a man name of Prentice during a poker game. But you never told me why."

It seemed that ever since the boy was old enough to hold a two-way conversation, he'd been fascinated with the facts surrounding his father's death. Kate had wanted to instill the picture of an upright man in Adam's mind, so he'd have a good example to follow. To accomplish that, she had no choice but to leave out most of the details.

"He was cheatin' at cards, wasn't he?"

"Oh, Adam," she'd begun, breathing a weary sigh, "you know this isn't my favorite subject. When will you—"

"When you tell me the whole story?"

Heart pounding, she'd stood, began stacking plates. "What makes you think I haven't?"

"Bobby heard his mother telling Kenny's mother that Pa was a gambler and a drunkard, that he got into lots of fights, and that he nearly killed a man once." Locking her into an intense gaze, he'd looked far older than he had a right to. "They say he hit you, too."

A butter knife clattered onto a plate. *Yes,* she'd thought, *there were beatings, and I still have the scars to remember them by. But what kind of mother would I be if I gave Adam memories like that about his father?*

Besides, it had happened years ago and miles away, in Raleigh. After the funeral, she'd packed their meager possessions and headed east, to start fresh on North Carolina's coast, where no one would know anything about Sean, or her or her son. How had Bobby's mother found out?

"Well," Adam pressed, "did he?"

She scrubbed a hand over her face. "Did he what, Adam?"

"Did he beat you?"

Another sigh. *Which is the greater sin,* she'd asked herself, *telling him a lie, or telling him what a beast his father was?* "Your father was—he was a colorful man," she'd said, choosing her words carefully.

"Not as colorful as you! They say he beat you black and blue."

Kate propped a hand on her hip. "Did Bobby get that from his mother, too? That woman needs to get out her Bible," she'd snapped, "and read James four eleven." She closed her eyes, " 'Speak not evil one of another, brethren. He that speaketh evil of his brother, and judgeth his brother, speaketh evil of the law, and judgeth the law: but if thou judge the law, thou art not a doer of the law, but a judge.' "

"I'm not a baby, Ma. You can tell me the truth."

"Have you done your chores?" she'd asked, hoping to change the subject.

"I'm not stupid, either," he'd added, shoving his chair back from the table.

From the moment of Adam's birth, everyone had commented on how much the boy resembled his father. At that moment, with the determined set of his jaw and the slight lift of his brows, he'd reminded her more of Sean than ever.

"I'm smarter than most kids my age; Miss Henderson said so last year in school. I'm smart enough to understand what—"

"I'm your mother, and I'll do what I think is best for you. And right now, it's best to drop this subject."

"But, Ma!"

"But nothing." With her fingertips, she had lifted his chin. "When I think you're ready for the truth, I'll tell you the rest."

"When will that be?"

Kate had pocketed her hand and looked away from the disappointment that had clouded his blue eyes. "I don't know, son. I only know that you're not old enough right now."

"I am so old enough!" And with a quirk of an eyebrow that was frighteningly reminiscent of his father, he'd folded both arms over his chest. "I'll bet you got in a few licks of your own, 'cause you're pretty good at defending yourself!"

Trembling with shock and rage, she had aimed a maternal digit at him: "Adam Flynn, I am your mother, and you will not speak to me that way, do you hear? Now, you march straight to your room, this instant!"

Slump-shouldered and grim-faced, he'd obeyed. And from that day on, he had begun spending more and more time with Bobby Banks, Currituck's resident troublemaker. Everything Adam had said after that had been argumentative; everything he'd done, rebellious. Just two days ago, flustered and furious, she'd pointed it out. And Adam had shrugged—something his father had always done—and said, "I'm half you, and I'm half him. What did you expect?"

The answer had not satisfied her. Quite the contrary. His words—spoken as if he were a young man of sixteen or eighteen instead of a lad of eight—had terrified her. What would become of her young son who, until now, had been playful, innocent, loving, and kind if he decided to emulate his father?

Now, alone in her dress shop, Kate sighed. Work was not taking her mind off her troubles, as it usually did. *Please, Lord, clear my mind of these burdensome worries. Either that,* she tacked on, grinning sardonically, *or give me the ability to worry while I work!*

She picked up a wedding headdress and started stitching candlewicked centers in the daisies she'd crocheted along its outer edges. When the flowers were complete, she'd attach them to a veil of sheer, gauzy white that would float all the way down to the gown's hem. It would be a lovely dress.

Kate wondered for the tenth time how Mr. Howard had secured enough satin for his daughter's big day. Times were hard, and fabrics like silk and satin and Spanish lace were all but impossible to come by. Somehow, he'd provided Kate with more than enough material to create the puffed sleeves, the full-circle skirt, and the billowing train.

"Why, Katie, I do believe that's the loveliest dress you've made so far."

She laughed softly. "You say that about every dress I make, Mary." Smiling at her elderly neighbor, she added, "I've got a kettle on the stove; how about a cup of tea?"

The old woman pulled out a chair and settled her considerable bulk into it. "Don't mind if I do," she huffed. "I've been on my feet since dawn!"

Kate fetched delicate china cups and saucers from the shelf above the big iron stove. "I guess you're here because Thaddius told you what happened this afternoon," she said, spooning tea leaves into the pot.

Mary nodded. "Don't you worry, sweetie. I raised seven young'uns of my own, don't forget. And like I always say, 'every last one of 'em gets ornery from time to time.' " She winked. "Adam's no exception; he's just testin' his wings, is all."

Kate shook her head, filled the cups with hot brew. "I hope you're right."

"Had me a favorite Bible verse when my boys were small," Mary said. She patted wayward wisps of hair back into her cotton-white bun, then held a forefinger aloft. " 'Take therefore no thought for the morrow,' " she recited, closing her eyes, " 'for the morrow shall take thought for the things of itself. Sufficient unto the day is the evil thereof.' "

Nodding, Kate smiled. "I'll add that one to 'Casting all your care upon him; for he careth for you.' "

Mary slurped noisily from the cup and pointed at the wedding gown. "Who's this one for?"

"Susan Howard."

"Ah, yes," Mary sighed, massaging her chins. "She's marrying Nathaniel Peters' youngest boy, if I'm not mistaken." Wiggling her eyebrows, she added, "It promises to be one of Currituck's biggest shindigs ever. You invited?"

"Yes, but I don't think I'll be going."

"Why ever not! You could use an afternoon off." Mary shook a maternal finger under Kate's nose. "You work too hard, if you ask me, Kate Flynn."

"Only hard enough to keep the wolf from the door."

"The wolf? Don't you mean the banker?"

"Wolf, banker, there's no difference if you ask me."

The old woman nodded. "Somethin' you'd know about better'n most, way I hear it."

The way you hear it? Kate repeated mentally. *Is the whole town talking about my past?* Suddenly, she had an idea: Everyone knew that Mary carried stories around town like a bee carries pollen. If Kate told the old woman the truth, Mary would dispatch the news faster than a *Gazette* reporter. *At least this way when the gossipmongers tell their tales, there'll be an ounce of truth in them.*

"It's strange," she began, smoothing the silky fabric that lay on her work table, "that my own wedding dress is the reason I'm a dressmaker today."

"Is that so?" Mary got up, waddled to the stove, and stirred a spoonful of sugar into her tea.

Kate nodded. "I was born in Philadelphia, you know, and so was Sean."

"Your husband?"

"Mmm-hmm. As a young girl, I thought he was so handsome, but he never paid much mind to me. At least, it never seemed that he noticed me. And then, I guess you'd say I grew up enough to realize that for all his good looks, Sean Flynn didn't have much good inside him, where it counted.

"His father got very sick when Sean was barely out of

college. He'd never exactly been poor, but when he put Sean in charge, the money started rolling in." Kate rolled her eyes. "My, but he could be ruthless. Foreclosures, evictions, refusals to loan money to the hard-working folks who really needed it."

Mary frowned. "Why would a sweet girl like you marry a man like that?" she wanted to know.

"Well," Kate said haltingly, "that's a rather long story."

Leaning forward, Mary's eyes twinkled with mischief. "Thaddius has had his supper."

For the next half hour, Kate kept Mary spellbound with the story of how her young brother had died of cancer ten years earlier. Treatments and medications, she continued, had all but depleted her parents' meager savings. When he died, the modest plot and nondescript headstone that marked his humble grave closed out the account.

"What a shame," Mary said, clucking her tongue. "Thank the Good Lord, me and my own have been blessed with everything we've needed, including good health." Shaking her head sympathetically, she added, "My heart goes out to your ma."

Kate nodded. "It was hard on my parents, on my mother in particular." She sipped her tea.

"And on you and your sister, too, I imagine."

"Yes," she said, remembering the heartache of watching her brother wither away, of watching his spirit leave him, of watching the plain pine box being lowered into the ground. "Yes, it was hard for us, too."

Mary sat forward in her chair, slapped her meaty thigh, and said in a grandmotherly voice, "So, your wedding dress got you started as a seamstress, did it?"

She was a kind woman, Kate knew, to try and lighten the mood with an abrupt change of subject. Trouble was, what Mary had heard so far was only the beginning.

"Yes, because I had to make my own, you see. My father

went to Sean, explained that he wouldn't be able to meet his bank note for several months, just until he secured enough business to get caught up on all the bills George's illness created. He was a carpenter, and no shirker. He would have been able to make the payments he'd missed, plus keep abreast of current notes due, if Sean had just given him a chance."

Mary blinked. "You don't mean to say—"

"He threatened to foreclose on the mortgage."

The old woman gasped. "Heartless!"

Kate nodded. She'd never told anyone the story before, so she had no idea the telling of it would be so difficult. *But if you don't finish what you've started, you'll always be haunted by the rumors. At least this way, women like Bobby's mother can spread the truth around for a change!*

Seated on the edge of her chair now, Mary leaned forward, clinging to Kate's every word. "He foreclosed?"

"He asked for my hand in marriage."

Rolling her eyes, the old woman's lips moved as she sent a whispered prayer heavenward. She met Kate's eyes. "Surely your pa didn't agree."

"No," she said. The word was no sooner out of her mouth than she was sliding back in time, remembering the conversation between her and her father:

"But Pa, why would I want to live my life with a hot-headed bully who divides his time between kicking good people off their property and beating people up in the saloon?"

Her father's cheeks reddened as he stared at the floor. "Aw, he's not as bad as all that, darlin'. Sean's just sowing some wild oats is all. Marriage will settle him down right quick." The smile never reached his eyes when he said, "Settled me down, didn't it?"

"You were never like Sean," she insisted. "Besides, what if marriage doesn't settle him down? What will become of me then?"

For a long moment, he said nothing, nothing at all. But

there was plenty he wanted to say. Kate could tell by the furrow of his brow, the flinching of his cheeks, the way his mouth formed a taut line. "You're right," he said at last, nodding. "I don't know what I was thinking."

Grateful to be free of the frightful marriage prospect, Kate threw her arms around him.

"It's your fault I'm so picky, Pa," she told him, kissing his whiskered cheek. "I want to marry a man just like you, loving and kind, hard-working, and—" She stepped back, laid a hand on his cheek and added, "and more handsome than the Shakespearean actors who came to town last year!"

Chuckling, he tweaked the tip of her nose. "You're full of stuff and nonsense, Katie Barnes. Now get on home and help your ma put supper on the table. I'm half starved!"

He turned back to his workbench, and continued carving a wood finial he'd add to the highboy he was building. Kate headed home.

During the mile-long walk between his workshop in town and their house, she asked herself why her father would try and talk her into marrying Sean Flynn in the first place. He knew as well as anyone the kind of reputation the banker had earned.

That night, Kate got her answer.

"Goodness, girl."

Mary's voice roused her from her reverie, returned her to the here and now.

"I thought you'd passed out or something," her old friend said, patting Kate's hand. "You were so quiet and still."

"I'm sorry. It's just I've never told anyone."

"I know, I know, sweetie," Mary said, giving her hand another pat. "But you can trust. . . Now, I know what some folks are sayin' 'bout me behind my back—that I'm a busybody and a talebearer—but if you'll notice," she said, a finger in the air, "the stories I tell ain't nothin' of any value." She pressed a stumpy fingertip to her temple. "You have no idea what-all is stashed away up here!"

And wouldn't that be ironic? she thought, sighing. *You open up for the first time in your life to set some facts straight and the so-called Gossip of Currituck won't spread the news!*

"So you made your own wedding dress, did you? The way you can work magic with a needle and thread, I'll bet it was a stunner!"

"It wasn't as lovely as this, but I walked down the aisle in white, at least."

"Oh, Katie."

She continued as if the woman hadn't spoken. "I realized if I didn't marry Sean. . ." Kate swallowed hard, remembering the heated argument she'd overheard between her parents. "He promised to cancel their debt, provided I agreed to become his wife. It was the only way out."

"Oh, Katie," Mary crooned, shaking her head, "you married a man you didn't love to save your family. You're a heroine!"

A heroine! She was nothing of the kind. Especially considering that the only reason she'd told Mary the story in the first place was to help her escape the gossip that was upsetting her son. She'd hoped that once the parents of the children who'd been talking to Adam about his father knew the truth, perhaps they'd instruct their youngsters to keep civil tongues in their heads, and go easy on her boy.

It had been a terrible idea, she realized. *If you hadn't gone off half-cocked, as usual. If you'd given it some forethought. If you'd asked the Lord's guidance in the matter.*

But it was too late. She'd already told Mary everything.

Well, almost everything.

She hadn't told her about the way Sean had smirked when she'd visited him at the bank the morning after hearing her parents' whispered argument to tell him if he was still interested, she'd marry him, nor how the smirk had changed to a sneer after they were married.

"Ma and Pa didn't have a penny to spare," she said, more

to hide from the dismal memories than to impart more information, "so I made my dress from a damask tablecloth my grandmother had given me." She smiled a little, remembering the way her sister had draped it over her shoulders before the sewing started, and how they'd collapsed in a fit of giggles over a string of horrible "table" puns:

"Well, you're all set," Susan said.

"I will be if you'll just pass me the scissors."

"You look like the salt of the earth, sister dear."

"After living all these years with you, marriage will be nothing but gravy!"

"It's good to know you enjoyed making the dress, at least," Mary said, interrupting her thoughts. "Just look at that smile on your face!"

"Yes, I enjoyed it." That, at least, was true.

"Did you make the veil out of this?" She touched the Spanish lace Mr. Howard ordered, all the way from Europe.

Kate couldn't help but laugh at that. "I should say not! My veil was made from the curtains Ma hung in my bedroom window. After the wedding, I made ruffles out of it, and sewed them to the collar and cuffs of the dress. A ribbon here, a ribbon there," she said, palms out, "and I had myself a Sunday go-to-meeting dress that I could wear all spring and summer!"

Kate drained the last of the tea from her cup, then told Mary how she became Mrs. Sean Flynn a month to the day after she'd accepted his proposal. "I was sixteen and he was thirty the day we moved into his room at his parents' house. And oh what a house it was!"

She described the many-roomed mansion, its ornate furnishings, the acres of rolling hillside surrounding it, the dozens of servants required to keep it all in order.

"Then one day about a month after we were married, Sean informed me we were moving. 'Heading south,' " she said, mimicking his deep, bossy voice, " 'because I can't stand living under my father's roof another minute!'

"He'd bought land in North Carolina, where he planned to start a whole new business venture: a chain of Flynn banks, one in every major city between Florida and New York. All he could say for months, it seemed, was 'We'll be rich, filthy rich!' "

"Did it work? Did he get rich?"

"Yes and no."

Mary's brow furrowed with confusion.

"Well, he made money, a lot of it. But he gambled it all away."

"Oh, Katie."

"I never wanted anything but a man who'd love me the way my pa loved my ma," she said, more to herself than to Mary. "As long as we had shelter, enough food, the basic comforts for our children, what did I care if we never got rich? The hardest part," Kate admitted, "was living so far from my family. I thought I might die of missing them."

In truth, her biggest fear had been that she'd die—period—during one of Sean's rages.

She remembered the first time he struck her.

She'd never been the shy, retiring type, but she did believe that her wifely duty was to show her husband respect, especially in public places. And so when Sean talked business at parties, after church services, to friends they met while walking down the street, she smiled and nodded to show that she supported him in what he said and did. Even when she could easily see that his latest plan (whatever it might be) was nothing but another pie-in-the-sky pipe dream, she did not question him in public.

She made the mistake of questioning him in private once.

"I don't want to go to Georgia," she'd blurted, a hand on her protruding belly. "I want our baby to be born here, in the home we built for—"

"You'll do as you're told," he'd said, turning his back to her.

If she hadn't been so upset, she might not have run around him, faced him head on. She might not have said, "My father never made major decisions without discussing them first with my mother."

His blue eyes glittered dangerously. "I am not your father, and you are certainly not the wife your mother is." He grabbed her wrist, jerked her against his chest and said through clenched teeth, "But you are my wife, and God help me, I'm stuck with you now." His eyes were mere slits when he added, "You're to give me obedience, not financial advice. If you ever question me again, you'll be sorry."

She'd been raised in a home where gentleness and love prevailed. How dare he put his hands on her as if she were an errant child! she'd thought. She'd been the best wife she knew how to be, especially considering the circumstances. Hurt, angry, humiliated, she issued a threat of her own: "If you ever talk to me this way again, you'll be sorry!"

A heartbeat later, she learned that when Sean issued a threat, he meant business, and for weeks, she stayed in the house to hide the stiffness and the bruises that were proof she'd learned the lessons well. Over time, Kate learned to accept the drunken binges and the beatings they inspired. What she had never come to terms with were the cold-blooded attacks that had not been whiskey-induced—the ones administered with no rhyme nor reason. Those beatings seemed to feed his sadistic pleasure, and sometimes, as she watched him come at her, Kate knew she was staring into the face of evil.

"Katie," Mary interrupted yet again, "you're pale as a bedsheet. Are you all right?"

Blinking, she focused on the here and now. "Yes. Yes, of course. I'm fine." Brightening, she said, "Now, where was I?"

"You were saying that you missed your family when Sean took you away from Philadelphia."

"Oh. Yes." And licking her lips, she continued, "Things got

progressively worse after that. The more money Sean made, the faster he spent it. We were in debt to our eyebrows, and he was forced to shut down six of the seven banks he'd opened. He took to gambling, saying if he was dealt just one good hand, he could fix everything that was wrong with his life."

"So that's how he got himself shot."

Kate's eyes widened. "How—how did you know about that?"

Mary shrugged. "Folks talk," was all she said.

Bobby's mother? she wondered. But what did it matter? She'd said so much, why stop now?

"Sean was desperate by then. The men who were in the game with him, others who'd been at the bar, testified that Harland Prentice accused Sean of slipping an ace of spades into the deck."

Mary shivered. "The death card."

Kate swallowed. She'd never heard it called that before. Still, "It was for Sean," she agreed.

"That's enough," Mary said, standing. "It's one thing to get things out in the open; it's entirely another to beat yourself with the memories." She pulled Kate to her feet and smothered her in a motherly embrace. "Put it out of your mind, sweetie," she whispered into Kate's ear. "He was a brute and a beast, way I hear it, and got his just desserts. When a man takes to whiskey and gambling, he's bound to end up in a bad way." Patting Kate's back, she added, " 'for all they that take the sword shall perish with the sword.' " Suddenly, Kate had an overwhelming need to be alone. Stepping away from the comfort of Mary's hug, Kate rubbed her temples.

Mary waddled over to the door and, one hand on the doorknob, faced Kate. "I meant what I said. I won't breathe a word of it to anyone. I promise."

Tears stung her eyes. Stubbornly, she blinked them back. "I never should have burdened you with—"

"Nonsense. Isn't healthy, keeping a thing like that all bottled up inside. It's a wonder you didn't pop like a party balloon!"

She felt like a weak, spoiled little girl, tattling on a schoolmate for taking her turn on the swing. "I haven't done anything to earn a friend like you, Mary."

Mary winked and yanked open the door. "Now then, why don't you turn in early? You've been lookin' a mite pale the last few days. The extra sleep will do you good."

"Maybe you're right."

" 'Course I'm right. I'm always right; just ask Thaddius!"

The women shared a brief round of laughter before Mary closed the door behind herself.

Kate looked at the ceiling. On the other side of it, her little boy lay sleeping. *Bless him with nothing but the sweetest dreams,* she prayed, *and protect him from harm, always. Protect him from—*

Her prayer was cut off by an internal question: *Why did you tell Mary all those things?* she demanded of herself. *Because you're spineless and self-centered, that's why; too weak to handle a little gossip, too weak to find the strength to learn to live with it. You had no business speaking ill of the dead, even if the man in question was a no-good, drunken. . .* She stopped herself. Whatever else he might have been, Sean had been Adam's father. And she'd move heaven and earth if need be to protect her boy from knowing what kind of man he'd been.

Because if the snippet of truth she'd given him a week ago had caused such a change in his behavior that he'd take to stealing, what would become of him if he found out about the things she'd just told Mary!

Kate slumped into the rocking chair near her work table and held her head in her hands. "What have you done?" she whispered. "What have you done?"

She could only hope that Mary had been telling the truth when she'd said many secrets lived in her head. Because if it had been a lie. . .

Folding her hands, Kate closed her eyes tight. *Forgive me, Father,* she prayed, *for coming to yet another important decision without first seeking Your guidance.* And in a small, trembling voice, she added, "Please don't let Adam find out about his father from anything I said tonight."

Heart hammering, she rose slowly and headed up the stairs.

She had a feeling sleep would be a long time coming tonight.

two

John Joseph O'Keefe lifted his hammer high, brought it down with a heavy hand, and secured the freeboard to the prow of the two-masted boat. Another week of work, and this fine little ketch would be ready for the wealthy New York entrepreneur who fancied himself a high seas skipper. It had taken a few weeks longer than normal to complete the project, since the rudder, the tiller, even the winches were attached so that its left-handed captain could manage the rigging with ease.

Behind him, the schooner he'd already finished sat waiting for pickup. It was an impressive sail craft, with jib-headed sails and extra-long turnbuckles. It had been one of his favorite projects, and J. J. was proud of the work. Not because he'd forged the cleats, cam-cleats, shackles, and other fittings himself, not even because he'd included double-strong goosenecks and mast hoops, but because he'd been given free rein to design the vessel's interior, allowing him to make full use of his carpentry skills. From cabin housing to hatch cover, from cockpit to companionway, every carefully-selected, cut and carved sheet of mahogany bore his artistic touch. And on the transom, the piece de resistance, the boat's name, bold and black and painted in J. J.'s one-of-a-kind lettering style: *The Flying Cloud*.

He loved his work, not only because it allowed him to make use of his hard-learned skills, but also because it allowed him to work alone. True, there weren't many one-man operations left—and he occasionally lost a job to a company whose multi-man crews could produce in record time—but J. J. refused to trade peace and privacy for pay. He could earn a great deal more by hiring his own multi-man crew. But what would he gain by hiring five men, or three, or even one to increase his output, if he lost the silent solitude he so treasured? Why, the normal day-to-day banter among workmen alone would cost him the sounds of the sea.

Sounds like the foghorn's mournful *phoomp-phoomp*, its two-note serenade punctuating the splash and hiss of the surf's spray, the gentle lapping of waves pummeling the pilings, the toll of a distant buoy bell.

He inhaled deeply of the salty air and, eyes closed, held the breath for a moment, relishing its prickly, briny scent. Smiling, he let it out, slow and easy.

He loved the sea, too, had always loved it.

J. J. knew that to some, it was a minacious, restless thing, deep and dark and dangerous, teeming with strange and monstrous beings that lurked beneath the surface, waiting to sink razor-sharp teeth into meaty flesh and brittle bone. But they saw only the violent, smoke-gray skies above it, streaked with sooty thunderclouds and silver-white lightning. Knew it as nothing more than a wild and wicked thing that churned the air into deadly williwaws that blew sailors and fishermen off course and into the waiting arms of Azrael.

It was all that, to be sure. But it was more, so much more.

To J. J., the sea was froth and foam and peaceful fog, and sweet-soft breezes that set halyards quietly clunking against masts—a syncopated melody that lulled him to sleep many a night.

And oh, how he loved the sea at night, when velvet-black skies sparkled with ten million pinpricks of starry light, and the water glinted from the milk-white glow of the moon. He loved it just as much in the daytime, too, when the golden glow of the daystar highlighted stout, swollen clouds and brightened the blue-green water, where, among sharp-toothed shark and stinging jellyfish, lived the playful dolphin.

Boats, ships, canoes—it didn't matter how large the vessel or how long it took him to build them—provided J. J. the only excuse he needed to be near his cherished waters. He knew men who compared the sea to a woman, citing quick-silver change as the reason.

Not J. J.

Oh, he'd always said things like "her" and "she" when refer-ring to it, of course. And yes, he was the first to agree that she was moody—tranquil one minute, stormy the next, destructive, disastrous, deadly even—but to compare her to a human female? In J. J.'s opinion, this was a dishonor she did not deserve.

The sea didn't behave as it did from a self-centered need to dominate. It did not consciously manipulate, nor calculatedly control the men who loved her. She had wiles, to be sure, that wooed and won men, but she never used them deliberately—as women used tears, pouting lips, sullen silences—to get her way.

She had no "way," but simply existed. A chemist might describe her as a complicated composition of chemicals and gases that, singly or in combination, reacted to things like gravity and atmosphere in a multitude of ways that had noth-ing whatsoever to do with man. But J. J. knew it was simpler than that. His presence, or lack of it, has no bearing on what she did or didn't do.

What a man saw when he looked into her dark, glittering waves could trick him, fool his eye if he let it. On days when she was turbid, no matter how hard or how long he scruti-nized her, he'd at best get a shallow glimpse of what hid beneath her gleaming, seemingly calm surface. But when the sun was bright and the sky clear, he oftentimes convinced himself he could look into the watery world and see all the way to the other side of the earth.

J. J. had experienced a similar sensation yesterday, looking into the Widow Flynn's wide eyes. He'd sensed there was more to her, far more, than she allowed the casual observer to see. And he'd had a feeling that even after careful observation, few would ever get to know the real Kate Flynn.

He hammered the last nail into the freeboard and ran a callused hand over the supple curve of the wood. Next, he'd finish up the championway, and after that, the foremast. One day soon, a sailor would climb the mast and, shading his eyes with a hand, he'd shout, "Boat on the horizon!"

"Where away?"

"Broad on the port quarter, Cap'n."

"Back the jib, then," he'd roar, reversing the tiller so the stern would swing to starboard. And as he prepared to bear off, he'd add, "Hard a'lee!" and steer through the eye of the wind.

The eye of the wind.

Now, why does that remind ye of Kate Flynn? he asked himself. *And why are ye thinkin' of her? She's not yer type. Not yer type a-tall.*

The only other brown-eyed woman he'd known up close and personal had been his mother. He didn't believe another had been born since who could match her in any way. Perhaps that was why the fair-haired types had always appealed to him. If J. J. hadn't learned anything else in his thirty-five years, it was the futility of fighting nature. He had a whole slew of relatives who had tried and failed. And the plain an' simple matter of it, he told himself, is that they're all dead as doorknockers this day because of it!

In the past, when he was drawn to a woman, it had been because of a pair of big blue eyes, waist-length blonde hair, a voluptuous figure, a smoldering, alluring voice. *The Widow has none o' those things in her favor, so why in tarnation has she been on yer mind night an' day since ye got yer first good look at her?*

Shrugging, he tried to focus on his work. *Maybe it's 'cause ye've got more'n a few things in common with her.*

For one thing, she'd come here seven years ago, after burying her husband. He hadn't been here long, himself. A hard winter's journey across the Atlantic had brought him to New

York back in '51. It had taken a year to work his way south, searching for a place he could call "home" after that hard journey across the Atlantic.

For another, he heard that she'd arrived with fifty dollars in her purse and nothing in her carpetbag but a change of clothes for her and another for the boy. J. J. had brought nothing from Ireland but an extra shirt, a few measly *punts*, and his journal.

Rumor had it she'd turned down three marriage proposals since setting up shop in Currituck, giving no reason other than she had a distaste for the institution. And J. J. had vowed, after what he now referred to as his only "close call," never to get closer than arm's length to a woman again.

And if that weren't enough, she'd paid cold hard cash for a building that had been half-destroyed by fire.

Many was the time he'd pass her window on his way to the feed and grain, and find himself fighting the temptation to stop and watch her, scrubbing the thick, sticky soot from the walls or, with saw and hammer and nails, replacing singed trimboards. And he'd built his warehouse with his own two hands.

If he hadn't seen it with his own two eyes, he might not have believed that she'd crafted and painted and hung the dress dummy-shaped sign outside her door. He'd designed his sign, too.

She'd set up shop on the first floor and set up house on the second.

He'd created a living space of sorts in the loft above the vast workspace. The only real fault gossipmongers could cite about her was that she spent far too much time at work and not nearly enough with her Bible. He certainly had no right to focus on that minuscule fissure in her character, when he hadn't been to church himself since long before he'd left Ireland. J. J. didn't know what kept her from the Scriptures, but he knew why he'd fallen from the fold:

As far back as the 1600's, one Royal Crown or another had

been degrading his people. Where had the Almighty been during the centuries when the English stole from his people their precious independence and their pride, leaving them only the harsh mistress of servitude? Where was the all-loving Father when the victories of Elizabeth the First meant the defeat of Ireland? Where was the powerful being when his ancestors were being starved, when their land was being stolen, their homes destroyed? Where was the good and merciful God when England ground Ireland into poverty and slavery? J. J. had lost everyone that mattered in the horrible potato famine— parents, siblings, aunts and uncles, cousins and neighbors. He had no use for a God who seemed to sanction all this wretchedness and misery.

He didn't know if Kate had even bothered to bring her Bible along when she left her sad past behind, but he knew that he had not.

What mattered was that she had packed up and left Raleigh, a place that, for her, was little more than painful memories, and sadness, and proof of foolish decisions. It had taken courage to do that. He knew, because he'd done it himself.

The differences? She'd left a city, he'd fled a disease-wracked homeland; he'd gone it alone, she done it with a young son in tow.

So where's all this comparin' and contrastin' takin' ye, O'Keefe? he asked himself. And in all honesty, J. J. had no answer.

If some other fellow had a mind to settle down, fine with him. As for J. J., he could cook and clean and darn his own socks. *What do I need with a woman, clutterin' up me house with knickknacks and doilies and bonnets and such?*

He'd satisfied his appetite for romance once, and it had left such a bitter taste that he doubted he'd ever hunger for it again.

'Course, if ye did have a mind to settle down, ye could do worse than Kate Flynn.

Frowning, J. J. shook his head to clear his mind of the cobwebs of the past and illusions of the present.

But even as he stepped over the schooner's rail and into the cabin, he had a feeling it would take more than any work he might do amidships to take his mind off the lovely widow.

❧

She'd seen him around town, dozens of times, heading to or from his warehouse, on his way in or out of Mary and Thaddius's feed and grain, walking alone along the dock. Kate hadn't given his solitary strolls much thought before their confrontational first meeting, but something stirred in her now, as she watched him moving slowly along the planking.

Kate had almost not purchased the narrow, two-story house with its twenty by fifteen-foot back yard. The clapboards had needed a good sanding and a fresh coat of paint, and there were shakes missing from the roof. The brick chimney certainly hadn't been cleaned in the years the dwelling had stood empty. Indeed, if the condition of the rest of the place was any indicator, it had likely never been brushed.

It had been a dreary afternoon when she'd first seen the house. As the driving rains pounded the ground outside, damp drafts slithered through cracks in the windowpanes, sneaked between floorboards, slid under the front door, cooling the spring air and cloaking Kate in gloom. She'd hugged herself, whether to fend off the chill or its accompanying ominous aura, Kate didn't know. To this day, she couldn't understand what had made her put one foot in front of the other to climb the charred, creaking staircase.

But to this day, she thanked God that she had.

For it had been as she stood in the window of the room that would be her own that Kate decided to invest the last of her savings in it.

Her gaze slid past the roof of the one-story house next door, past the barn-like structure beside it, and traveled to sea. She could not tear her eyes from it, because, despite the gunmetal gray sky, the howling wind, the drenching downpour, the view was like nothing she'd ever seen.

The Atlantic's choppy wavetips glowed, as if each had been streaked with white by an artist's paintbrush. Between the thick, smoky clouds that rumbled overhead, patches of pearly white peeked through. And the mist that rolled lazily toward shore hovered around the dock workers' feet like ashes that had been disturbed by a whiff of air.

If the sea can look this beautiful in weather like this, she'd told herself, think what it'll be like on a bright sunny day.

That view alone had been worth every splinter, every blister, every stiff joint and sore muscle that had resulted from the arduous hours of turning the house into a home for Kate and her son. Though it was ever-changing, always different, the scene was the constant in her life, the one thing she could count on to lift her sagging spirits, renew her faith. She came to depend so greatly on its restorative powers that Kate placed a high-backed rocker and a small table near the window, so that when life threatened to overpower her, she could sit facing the ocean's shore. Later, she'd had a small porch built, so she could step outside to enjoy even more of the view, unhampered.

Without fail, the majestic panorama would calm her, soothe her, remind her Who had created the awesome beauty before her. *If He could do this,* she'd tell herself, *He can ease your petty fears.*

"Going to the Window," she called it in the privacy of her mind. She'd gone there today to think and pray about Adam's behavior of late, to seek the Lord's guidance in how to handle the boy's unruly, cantankerous moods. A gentle May breeze filtered through the open window, lifting the gauzy white curtains, riffling her golden-brown hair.

Resting both elbows on the sill, she propped her chin in a palm, took a deep breath, and closed her eyes to savor the spring-flower fragrance. When she opened them, she saw him, head down and hands pocketed, standing alone on the dock. He withdrew one hand, drove it through his hair, then let the arm fall limp at his side. His shoulders lifted, fell, and she took it as a sign that he, too, had inhaled the sweet scent of the sea. He turned slightly, tilted his bearded face toward the sky, and shook his dark-haired head.

She knew very little about him, save that he'd used his fists to buy everything that was his. Well, that wasn't entirely true. She also knew that he'd come to Currituck by way of New York after fleeing the fever and the famine in Ireland. Of course, if it hadn't been for Thaddius, she'd know nothing of the kind. Indeed, she'd know nothing about any of the town's inhabitants, except perhaps the measurements of the ladies whose dresses she designed. Always one to give credit where credit is due, Kate admitted that her neighbor's lips loosened only when he sipped too long from the bottle of tonic Doc Peterson had prescribed, which was no fewer than twice a week. Where he secured the information he passed on was anyone's guess, but she supposed that as long as she didn't pass any of the so-called news along, it wasn't the same as gossiping.

According to Thaddius's reports, J. J. O'Keefe had never lost a match. Not that it surprised her. Even a man as big and broad as John Joseph O'Keefe would be hard-pressed to beat him, for most lacked the initiative and the energy to be a champion. She could see in his no-nonsense stance, in his matter-of-fact way of speaking, in his straightforward way of looking everyone in the eye that he had what it took to be a champion.

After each victory, Thad had said, O'Keefe allowed himself a small reward: a restaurant meal in the nearest big city, siphoning off just enough from his winnings to pay for his room at whichever boarding house he was calling home at the time. Once he settled in Currituck, he spent every non-boxing moment up on Buck Bay, working for Emmit Creed on his fishing trawler. Every penny he earned, fishing or fighting, the old man reported, went into the bank. Within a year, he'd saved enough to buy the property near the dock, and the wood and nails to build his warehouse. *What is it about Irishmen,* she wondered, *that drives them so? What is it that makes them want to be the best? To drink and fight and—* Sean had had that same determination to succeed, those same ambitious dreams. When he was in one of his get-ahead moods—which was most of the time—he wore the same arrogant, all-knowing, "I can do anything" expression that had been plastered on O'Keefe's face the day he'd blown into her shop like a tornado.

Kate remembered the way he'd branded her with that gray-eyed stare, as if he could read her mind and her heart and her soul with one searing glance. She shuddered involuntarily, for if he had been able to read her at all, he'd have known that his mere presence had awakened fears she'd thought long-since buried.

Now, she watched O'Keefe lean his backside on a thick, burled piling, cross both arms over his chest, and lower his bearded chin. Her brow furrowed as she leaned farther out the window for a better look. *Could he be praying?* she asked herself. *No, of course not; he doesn't seem the type.* But then, hadn't she heard that the Irish were religious by nature and by birth? Sean had certainly turned to the Lord on more than one occasion.

Pity it was only when he'd exhausted his money gambling or his energy pounding on me!

Elbows pointing north and south and palms flat on the windowsill, Kate rested her chin on the backs of her hands and sighed deeply. She didn't understand the emotions rising in her as she continued to watch him, down there, alone on the dock. Something in him seemed to be calling out to something in her, a heartfelt, desolate plea that told her he was as lonely—and as tired of being lonely—as she. True, he'd huffed and pawed like an angry bull that day when Adam stole his lunch, but then, his privacy had been disturbed, his property violated. Hadn't he had every right to be riled?

The day Adam stole his lunch.

She exhaled another sigh. "What are you going to do with that boy of yours?"

As if he'd heard her whispered question, O'Keefe's head came up and, without looking left or right, he focused directly on her. For a long, eerie moment, they remained locked in the unnerving eye-to-eye connection. She likened the link to a spider's web, strong enough to house the arachnid, yet fragile enough to be torn from its moorings by a gust of wind.

When at last the moment ended—and it ended only because he looked away—Kate thought she understood how the eight-legged creature might feel when the silken lattice-work that took hours, days to construct, was quickly and cruelly destroyed without warning. The eye contact between Kate and J. J. had lasted two, perhaps three, blinks of an eye, more than long enough for her to acknowledge that during that tick in time an awareness of one another had bound them, mind to mind, soul to soul.

He glanced upward again, tilted his head to one side, pocketed both hands.

Is he—? Is he smiling? she wondered. *Yes, yes I believe he is smiling!* Flustered that she'd been caught—again!—ogling him, Kate straightened her back, and moved away from the window.

It was a distance of perhaps fifty yards from this spot to the docks below. Too far to see a woman in a window? *Of course it's too far, she told herself. Maybe he didn't see you, staring— no, brazenly gawking is more like it. Maybe it only seemed as though he was boring straight through you.*

Boring through her and straight into her heart with that all-knowing gray gaze of his.

She'd never been one to take comfort from false hopes,

whether large or small. There was no consolation in pretending the spell-binding moment hadn't happened. No consolation in pretending he hadn't seen her. Standing, Kate smoothed her apron, tucked a wayward tendril of hair into her bun, and backed further away from the window.

She and J. J. O'Keefe had lived in the same town for years. Although nothing more than a squatty building separated their businesses, their homes, and their lives, their paths had never crossed, so neither had had occasion to do speak to the other before Adam's thievery.

For a reason she accepted (for surely she didn't understand it!), chance meetings had a way of repeating themselves. Sooner or later, Kate believed, she and John Joseph O'Keefe would bump into one another again. When they did, she hoped the encounter would not be angry or confrontational. But whether it was or it wasn't, how would she deal with the fact that she was strangely attracted to the Irishman? Especially since she'd made a promise, on behalf of Adam and herself, never to get close to a man again?

≈

She rode into town on a white pony, head held high and eyes straight ahead.

"Who is she?" Mary whispered to Thaddius.

"You've got me by the feet, Mother," came his quiet response.

Mary took a step closer to her husband. "She looks like an Indian."

"Well," he said, moving his briar pipe from one side of his mouth to the other, "she's got all the look of a squaw."

"But she's wearing a white woman's dress, and high-heeled boots on her feet. What do you make of that!"

"There's your answer right there, Mother," he said, pointing to the woman's shoes with the stem of his pipe. "No Indian in her right mind would trade those comfortable moccasins for hard-soled boots."

She reined in the beast when she drew parallel to the feed and grain, dismounted, and tethered him to the iron ring hanging from the hitching post. "I am in need of flour and corn meal," she calmly announced. "Do you have these things?"

"Y—yes, yes, why of course we do," Mary stammered. Lifting her skirts, she started up the steps. "Won't you come inside and—"

The woman held up a silencing hand. "Before you go to much trouble," she began, "I must tell you I have no American dollars. I hope to trade for what I need."

Laying a fat-fingered, wrinkled hand upon her bosom, Mary looked at Thaddius. "Well, now, I don't know. We've always done a cash-only business."

Her husband stepped forward. "Nonsense," he said, frowning, "what kind of fool waltzes into town, expectin' somethin' for nothin'? We can't start tradin' baubles and beads for our goods. How would we—"

The woman reached onto her horse's back, removed the small burlap sack hanging from the saddle horn. Opening its drawstring mouth, she dipped one hand inside. "Are these what is known as 'baubles and beads' in your town?" she asked, extending her hand, palm up.

Thaddius took a step forward, and with a gnarled forefinger, poked at one of the gemstones she held. "Are they diamonds?"

One corner of her mouth lifted in a wry grin. "I could say that they are—I can see you would not know that diamonds do not grow in North Carolina soil." Inclining her head slightly, she added, "But Running Deer does not lie." She smiled. "They are crystals. I polish them myself."

"Beautiful," Mary sighed, blue eyes glittering greedily.

"And those?" Thaddius asked, pointing.

"Iron."

"But it's gold!"

She nodded. "Some call it 'fool's gold,' and for good reason. Its true name is pyrite," she explained. "It is harder, but not as heavy as the real thing. And do you see these grooves, here?"

Thaddius nodded.

"Real gold would have no such grooves."

He regarded her from the corner of his eye. "How is it you know so much about it?"

Laughing softly, she dropped the stones back into the bag. "A missionary taught me to read and write. Taught me to cipher numbers, too. I learned it from a book."

"Why, that's wonderful," Mary exclaimed, clamping her hands together. "Did you learn about our Lord Jesus from the missionary?"

Another nod. "Yes."

"Well," Mary coaxed, "did you invite Him into your heart? Did you accept Him as your Lord and Savior?"

"I did."

"Good for you!" she said, clapping. "Was your whole tribe saved?"

The friendly smile disappeared, the warm light in her dark eyes vanished. She shook her head.

"Why ever not?" Thaddius demanded. "Do they want to go to heaven when they die, or not?"

The question induced a small grin. "They believe in a different god, but they believe."

"Ain't no god but the One True God," Thaddius proclaimed.

"I am convinced, but they could not be."

The elderly gent narrowed his eyes, rubbed his double chins between thumb and forefinger. "What tribe are you with, anyway?"

"I have no tribe."

"Nonsense. You're an Indian, ain't you? 'Course you have a tribe."

She hung the gem sack on the saddle horn once more and glanced off to the west as a sad, faraway look crossed her face. "Once," she said, her voice barely more than a whisper,

"I was of the Algonquin people."

"You sayin' you ain't one now?"

She took a deep breath. "Yes."

"Why ever not?" He frowned, squinted. "Say, you didn't kill nobody, did you?"

Pursing her lips, she arched one brow. "Not yet."

The old man's blue eyes widened and his jaw dropped.

"What's all the chattering about?" Kate asked, smiling as she stepped onto the porch of her shop. "You sound like a couple of magpies out here, going on about."

"I am Running Deer," the Indian woman announced, bowing slightly at the waist. "I came in the hopes that I could trade for flour and corn meal." Her dark gaze found Mary's eyes, Thaddius's, then returned to Kate's. "It seems I have come a long way for nothing."

Kate had heard the word "bigotry," and certainly could define it as well. But never before had she seen it put into practice, right before her very eyes. It surprised her that her friends and neighbors—people she thought she knew and understood—could judge any human being because of the color of her skin.

"What's going on here?"

Kate's heart thundered at the sound of Howard Anderson's booming voice. He was Currituck's resident bully and troublemaker. As if Running Deer hadn't already been through enough!

"What're you doing, passing the time of day with one of them redskins?" he demanded. "Don't you know their skin is crawling with critters? Haven't you heard they're murdering, thieving—"

"Good morning, Howard," Kate interrupted. It was a shame, she'd always thought, that such Nordic good looks had been wasted on this shallow, conceited man. But perhaps his vanity had a purpose other than to annoy those around him. "Where have you been keeping yourself?" she asked, forcing a brightness into her voice that she didn't feel. "I haven't seen you at Sunday services in weeks and weeks."

"Why, good morning yourself, Mrs. Flynn." He removed his Derby and, smiling, said, "I've been busy. Might just stop by this Sunday, though."

"How is Adelaid?"

At the reminder of his wife, Howard put his hat back on. Minus the smile, he answered, "She's fine. Just fine."

"And the children?"

"Good. Real good."

"Seems the only time I see you these days is when you come into the shop to order a new shirt or suit." She'd made him a dozen shirts, half as many pairs of trousers, and two suits in the years she'd known him, and could remember altering two dresses for his wife. She rolled her eyes. "Work, work, work!" she said.

"You a part of this little hen party?" Howard wanted to know.

" 'Hen party'?" She furrowed her brow. "I'm afraid I don't—"

He nodded toward Running Deer. "Is she visiting you, too?"

"She ain't visitin' us!" Thaddius put in. "The woman wanted to trade rocks for some supplies. I told her 'no deal.' She was just about to leave," he glared at her, "weren't you?"

Running Deer stared at her feet, and shook her head slowly. From the look on her face, it was plain to Kate she'd grown accustomed to this type of treatment.

"Actually," Kate said, taking the horse's reins, "she was just about to come with me." She met the woman's eyes. "Weren't you, Running Deer?"

Suspicion glinted in her dark, slanting eyes, but she allowed Kate to lead her away, stopping to untie her pony and lead it along. Kate waved to Mary and Thaddius. "See you two later."

As she turned the corner, she smiled at Howard. "Say hello to Adelaid for me."

The trio murmured quietly as the women drew out of sight. When they reached the dress shop's back door, Kate tethered Running Deer's horse to the railing, grabbed the metal bucket from the porch's top step, and proceeded to pump it full of water. "There!" she said, giving her hands a satisfying dusting, "that ought to hold him for a while." She looked at the animal's owner. "Or is it a she?"

"His name is Konawa."

"Konawa." She patted the horse's rump. "What does it mean?"

" 'Barter,' " Running Deer explained, "or 'deal.' "

"I imagine you made a good trade for him."

Running Deer smiled, and so did Kate. "Konawa will be fine out here for now. I have an apple and some oats I can give him in a little while, but won't you join me upstairs first?" She didn't wait for a response. Instead, she hiked up her skirt front and hurried up the steps.

Running Deer hesitated only a moment before following. From the kitchen doorway, she said, "I do not know whether you are a very brave woman, or a very stupid one."

Kate stopped pumping water into the tea kettle long enough to meet the woman's eyes. "Neither, I hope," she said, smiling at the teasing grin on her face. She struck a match, lit the coals under the stove plate, and, wiping her hands on her apron, invited Running Deer to sit.

She chose the chair nearest the door, sat stiffly erect, and folded her hands on the table top. "Are you always this kind, or have you made an exception. . ." she paused, "on my behalf?"

Grinning, Kate sat across from her. "I must have made an exception for you, because if you want the truth, I don't ordinarily have time for polite conversation or pleasant exchanges."

Her comment inspired the first of many smiles she would coax from the Indian woman, and before the night was over, Kate felt she had made a friend, the first she'd had since leaving Philadelphia.

&

For the first time in weeks, Adam's behavior was something other than grumpy and mean. "I liked Konawa," he told his mother at breakfast the next morning. "He let me feed him apple slices, you know."

"Running Deer tells me he isn't friendly with most people. She says you must be very special."

When he smiled, his whole face lit up. Oh, how she'd missed seeing the deep dimples in his freckled cheeks!

"Is she coming back soon?" he said around a mouthful of toast.

"She didn't say, but I hope so."

"You haven't had a lady friend in a long time, have you, Ma?"

Kate felt the heat of a blush creeping into her cheeks. "No. I don't suppose I have."

"Why not? You're the prettiest woman in Currituck, and the nicest, too."

Her flush deepened and her heartbeat quickened in response to the boy's compliment. "What a nice thing to say, Adam. Thank you."

He shrugged. "It's the truth, that's all," he said matter-of-factly. His nonchalant expression turned serious when he added, "Ma, can I ask you something?"

"You know you can."

Adam nodded. "I was just wondering." His young brow furrowed as he considered his next words. "Would you be angry with me if I, um, if I went to work for Mr. O'Keefe?"

"Are you sure?"

"Yes, Ma, because he was right, you know."

"About what?"

"About not being able to get any sleep, on account of I'd feel bad about what I did. I don't like feeling guilty. I have a conscience, Ma, I do!"

"Of course you have a conscience. Whatever made you think you didn't?"

He leaned a cheek on a doubled-up fist. "Well," he began, poking his fork tine into the skin of his fried egg, "I just did things before, you know, without thinking about what other folks might think—if it made 'em angry, or hurt their feelings, or. . ."

"You've been thinking about all that, just because of what Mr. O'Keefe said?"

Adam nodded. "Uh-huh." He sat up straight. "So can I, Ma? Can I work at the warehouse, to pay for the lunches I stole?"

She took a sip of her coffee, more to forestall the tears than to figure out what she'd tell her son. *He's growing up,* she admitted, *he's becoming a man—thanks to John Joseph O'Keefe!*

three

Adam took a deep breath and squared his shoulders. "I'm sorry, Mr. O'Keefe."

J. J. did his all-fired best to hide the smile that had been bubbling inside him since he'd first noticed the boy, crouching in the warehouse doorway as if a rabid dog was on the loose. As Adam continued searching for him, looking right and left outside the building, a gull had screeched overhead. Both of the boy's feet left the ground in startled response. Arms akimbo and neck craned, he appeared to be straining his ears to identify the sound. The gull swooped low, squawked again, and Adam ran a hand through his dark curls. J. J. could almost hear the boy heave a relieved sigh.

'Tis yer fault the little fella fears his own shadow, O'Keefe, he thought as the boy stood before him now, twisting his short-billed cap in his hands. *'Tweren't never my intention,* he told himself, *to frighten the boy.*

Well, that wasn't completely true. He'd been miffed when his first lunch disappeared. Annoyed when the second one vanished. When he watched the third being carried off by the trio of hooligans, it had riled him. *But why waste yer time on a pack of scruffy ruffians,* he'd asked himself. *They're bound for prison no matter what ye say.*

It had been the flash of fear and dread, shining in the youngest boy's eyes that inspired J. J. to give chase. The guilty "Oh, no!" expression told him that maybe that boy, at least, could be saved. As a lad, J. J. had had a similar experience. *If not for old man McPherson,* he reminded himself, *there's no tellin' how ye might have ended up.*

Now, his heart went out to Adam, standing before him on

the dock, looking up at him with wide, worried eyes. J. J. fought the urge to throw down his sandpaper, pull the boy into a hearty hug, and promise that all was forgiven. But he could see by Adam's quivering lower lip, could hear in his trembling voice how hard it had been to come here. *'Tis a manly thing he's trying to do,* he told himself. *He's earned a moment of dignity.*

He leaned both forearms on the freshly-sanded rail. "Sayin' yer sorry, hard as it is, is all well and good, providin' ye mean it," he began in a soft, steady voice. "The hard part is provin' it." He paused. "What d'ye have in mind?"

Adam took a deep breath. "Well," he began, "I've been thinking about what you said." He gave the cap another twist, glanced furtively toward the walkway leading away from the dock toward freedom.

To his credit, the boy stood his ground. Straightening his narrow back, he said, "I want to pay what I owe."

The matter-of-fact voice seemed to have surprised him, because once the words were out, he glanced about as if in search of the fellow who'd said it. When he realized it had been his voice that had sounded so strong and sure, a tiny smile lifted one corner of his mouth, and pride stood him taller still.

It was all J. J. could do to keep from chuckling under his breath. Bending closer to his work lest Adam see the merry gleam in his eye, he asked, "Does yer ma know ye're here?"

Adam nodded. "Yes, sir."

"She's in favor of yer workin' off the debt, then?"

Another nod. "We had a long talk about it last night."

J. J. put the sandpaper into his bucket of supplies and, straightening, leaned both palms on the rail. *Ah, but the woman has her hands full, what with workin' to support the boy, and doin' all the usual motherin' things as well.* In a swift, smooth movement, he swung himself over the rail, and landed on the dock with a solid thunk. Adam's eyes widened and he took a careful step back.

"Ye're a lad of many moods, aren't ye?"

Adam's cap was an unrecognizable tangle as he wrinkled his nose in confusion. "Sir?"

"Ye weren't standin' tall the day ye stole me lunches. Ye didn't speak like a lad with proper breedin', either." He smiled a bit. "Why, ye had me convinced the lot of ye were murderous punks, just out of prison, ye did!"

Adam looked at the toes of his boots. "I'm not with those boys anymore."

"Why ever not?"

"My ma says folks will judge me by the company I keep." Without raising his head, he peeked through long lashes at the Irishman. "I don't want folks thinking I just got out of jail."

She's a good ma, tellin' him things that're no doubt as hard to say as they are to hear. They were things a father should have been telling his son. J. J.'s heart ached for her and went out to the child who reminded him so much of himself as a youth. Crouching, he pretended to rub a scuff from his boot. "When would ye like to start?"

Adam licked his lips. "Right away, sir."

He remained child-sized to ask, "D'ye know how to handle a hammer?"

"Yes, sir. I have my own tool box," he said, smiling for the first time since they'd met. "When things come loose around Ma's shop, I'm the one who whacks 'em back into place." He punctuated his statement with a proud jerk of his chin. "Got me a cross saw, and a pry bar, and a—"

"How 'bout a level and a T-square? And how's your arithmetic?"

"Arithmetic? I hate arithmetic!"

"The hand that wields the tool is no better than the head that guides it."

Adam tucked in one corner of his mouth, nodding in half-hearted agreement.

Chuckling, J. J. placed a hand on the boy's shoulder. "I think it's best we don't put any strain on yer tools, since ye need 'em to help out yer ma and all. You'll use mine, and I have plenty, as you'll soon see."

The fear that had been glinting in Adam's eyes when he first approached was gone now. Slowly, J. J. stood. "Ye'll give me three hours: one for each lunch. Fair enough?"

"Yes, sir."

J. J. extended his hand. For an instant, the boy hesitated. He recovered quickly, though, and thrust out his arm, his hand all but disappearing in J. J.'s big one as they shook on it.

J. J. spent the next half hour giving Adam a tour of the warehouse, the dock, the boats he was building, the one he'd just finished. The boy paid wide-eyed attention, nodding, asking questions, repeating proper boating and building terms. *He'll be all right,* J. J. told himself, *if he keeps away from those hoodlums.*

At the conclusion of the tour, he opened his shiny new lunch bucket and unwrapped a cheese sandwich. After handing half to Adam, he grabbed two mugs from the shelf above the coal stove. "D'ye drink coffee, lad?"

Adam held the mug J. J. handed him as if it were made of solid gold. "No sir, but I've always wanted to try."

He hesitated, holding the pot over the mouth of Adam's mug. "It's only fair to warn ye, I'll not go again' yer ma."

"She doesn't have anything against coffee." Adam tucked in one corner of his mouth. "At least, I don't think she does."

"Ye don't think so?"

"Well, she's a tea drinker."

Smiling, J. J. filled Adam's mug halfway. "It gets a bit ripe by this time of the mornin', I'm afraid. Sorry I haven't any milk to cut the taste." He put the speckled metal pot back on the stove and took a swig from his own mug.

Adam mimicked his movements, right down to the satisfied "Ah" that punctuated J. J.'s swallow. "I knew I'd like it," he said.

"Y'don't say."

He met J. J.'s eyes. "It always smelled like it'd taste good."

If he'd affectionately mussed the boy's curls when the urge struck on the dock earlier, the action might have seemed insulting to the boy. He didn't believe there was any danger of that now, so J. J. roughed-up Adam's hair. "Bring yer coffee with ye," he said, ambling toward the workbench, "and let's get busy."

It seemed he had grown a three-foot shadow, which could only mean one thing: Adam wanted a man's firm hand every bit as much as J. J. knew he needed it.

Did he want to be that man?

Ye'd best make up yer mind right quick, O'Keefe, he warned himself, *'cause if you get involved now, ye'll likely be in it to yer armpits for a long, long time.*

Did he have the time?

Yes and no.

But did he want to make the time, or exercise the patience that would be required to teach the emotionally unsteady youngster about carpentry, about shipbuilding, about life?

And what about the boy's mother? *She was fit to be tied when I insinuated she wasn't doing such a hot job raising her boy. It'll be like tanglin' with a mama tiger, for sure.*

Could he deal with that?

Did he want to even try?

He glanced at Adam, found the boy looking up at him with wide eyes that beamed with boyish innocence. *How long is that likely to last,* J. J. asked himself, *without a man to keep him in line?* He hesitated, wavering for an instant between protecting his beloved solitude and helping this needy boy.

J. J. took a deep breath and put his mug on the workbench. Lifting his bearded chin, he crossed both arms over his chest. "Well, are ye ready for yer first assignment?"

"Yes, sir."

"All right then, listen up."

Adam copied J. J.'s stance, opened his eyes wider to prove he was paying attention.

"Stop callin' me 'sir,'" J. J. said. "Makes me feel like a doddering old fool."

Adam's brows rose on his forehead. "Yes, sir. I mean, Mr. O'Keefe."

Gently, he chucked the boy's chin, inspiring a smile that would have lit the whole room. "And not 'Mr. O'Keefe,' either. The name's J. J. Got it?"

Smiling, Adam grinned. "Got it."

Someday, perhaps he'd tell the boy about his experience with Nate McPhereson. For now, J. J. could only hope he was man enough to do for Adam what the old man had done for him.

❧

"Yer boy was admiring this today," he said, standing a careful distance away, "when I showed him 'round the warehouse."

Kate stepped forward to accept the tiny replica of a many-masted sailing vessel, accurate to the most minute detail. "It's beautiful," she admitted.

"'Tis nothin','" he said, shrugging. "I don't usually make 'em for the smaller boats, but when I get a contract to build somethin' more elaborate, I put together a scale model."

She turned it around, studied it from that angle. "I'll bet some folks say it's a lot of unnecessary work, don't they?"

"As a matter of fact, some do."

"There's no doubt it is a lot of extra work, but it's not the least bit unnecessary. I understand exactly why you do it."

"Oh, ye think so, do ye?" he asked, grinning.

Returning his playful smile, she nodded. "This is much more intricate, of course, and takes far more skill, but in theory, it's a pattern. Like the ones I draw up before sewing a dress or a suit." She held the boat out to him. "It's nice to have something to look at when you get down to work."

" 'Tisn't often I run into a body—'specially a female body—who understands why I do some of the things I do." He smiled. "But I didn't bring the boat over here to show it off, though it's right pleasant to get yer opinion on it."

Statue-still, she held the boat to her breast. "Then why did you bring me the boat, Mr. O'Keefe?"

Cupping his chin in a palm, he regarded her carefully. "Ye seem like a no-nonsense woman to me. Am I right?"

"I'll admit I've never had much respect for people who don't say what they mean. It's a colossal waste of time, for one thing, and then there's always a chance people will misunderstand your intention."

"I'll take ye at yer word, then, and say it straight out: The boat isn't for you. It's for yer boy."

Smiling, she thanked him. "I'm sure he's going to treasure it always."

"Somethin' else, ma'am."

Kate's brows rose as she waited for him to say what was on his mind.

"Would ye mind very much callin' me 'J. J.'? I hear 'Mr. O'Keefe' and I expect to see me da nearby, 'cause in me head, he's the only legitimate 'Mr. O'Keefe'!"

My but he's handsome when he smiles that way, Kate thought. *It's a shame he doesn't do it more often.*

The smile became a grin as he held a thumb and forefinger inches apart. "So tell me, Missus Flynn, do ye have wee duplicates of all the dresses ye've made?"

It made her blush to admit that, on occasion, in addition to making patterns, she had sewn doll-sized versions of her creations. "How did you know?"

He shrugged. "Ye look like the type, that's all."

"What type?"

"Ye know," he said offhandedly, "a woman who's made a place for everything, who can't let a speck of dust settle without gettin' the feather duster out, who—"

"The woman you're describing sounds like a fanatic, Mr. O'Kee—I mean, J. J.," she interrupted. "And I am not a fanatic!"

Grinning, he leaned closer and whispered, "That's not what yer boy says."

Since Sean's death, being this near a man made her flinch, as though still half expecting to dodge a fist or shut her ears to a cutting remark. For a reason she couldn't explain, J. J.'s nearness caused no such anxiety. Quite the contrary. His presence made her feel safe. Protected. She inclined her head, smiled, and in a soft voice, asked, "What does my boy say?"

She watched J. J.'s gray eyes darken, his left brow rise, the corner of his mouth lift in a wry grin in reaction to her innocent flirtation. "He says if he puts a thing down, even for one tick of the clock, ye're off and runnin' with it." Chuckling, he added, "He says he doesn't know where most of his things are."

Giggling, Kate harumphed, and crossing her arms over her chest, said, "Why, they're—"

"Right where they belong, of course!" they said together, laughing.

A moment of companionable silence passed before she said, "I was just about to have a cup of tea. Would you like some?"

He grinned. "Well, ordinarily, I'm a coffee drinker."

She hardly knew what to make of it, because one moment he was Irish, through and through, and the next he could have been a member of Parliament: "But I wouldn't mind a brisk cup of tea, madam."

Kate had grown up hearing proper British accents, since her mother's parents had been born and raised in Barrow, a small seaport on England's Morecambe Bay. "Won't you join me inside, then?" she asked, curtseying before leading him up the stairs and into her apartment.

Once inside, J. J. looked around. "I was right," he said, nodding approvingly.

She pumped water into the tea kettle. "Right about what?"

"I'd wager I could eat off this floor, it's so clean, and there's not a scrap of clutter anywhere in sight."

The admiration in his voice and in his eyes was obvious. Still, it puzzled her. Why wouldn't the home she'd made for her son be clean and tidy? The world outside was fraught with disorder and upheaval; wasn't it her duty to provide her son with a haven from that chaos? Life was unpredictable, at best; wasn't it her responsibility to see that his home was a safe harbor from the tumult? "A house is just a house if things aren't organized, Mr. O'—ah, J. J. A house isn't a home until a mother's love makes it so."

She couldn't identify the expression that crossed his face in response to her statement. Kate chalked it up to the fact that he was a bachelor.

As she set the table and poured the tea, they discussed the weather, the clock tower the town elders wanted to build in the center of town, and the upcoming church social. And then Kate blurted out the question that had been niggling at her since she'd first noticed him, hovering around the back steps. "Tell me, J. J., what really brings you here?"

His beard hid very little of his blush as he pointed to the little boat. "Why, the model, of course."

"Adam is working for you now," she said, taking a seat at the table. "You could have given it to him yourself." Her gesture invited him to sit, too.

J. J. turned the chair around, swung one leg over its seat as if mounting a short-legged horse. Grinning, he leaned both forearms across the chair's back and met her eyes. "Ye're not one to mince words, are ye, Missus Flynn?"

"It's a waste of time," she said again, and lifting the cup to her lips, added, "But you haven't told me why you're here."

J. J. cleared his throat. "I only meant to leave the boat outside yer door, so the boy would find it first thing in the morning. I never expected ye'd be out on the porch on such a cool night."

Kate often stood looking out to sea before getting ready for bed. It soothed her, steadied her nerves. Until J. J., no one but she knew it.

"You seemed a million miles away." He paused. "Where was it ye were wishin' to be?"

She laughed softly. "Oh, it was nothing as melodramatic as that. It's just–it's just that the sound and the scent of the water calms me."

"Hasn't been easy for you, has it?"

Smiling wistfully, she glanced in the direction of her slumbering son's room. The smile faded under his intense scrutiny. Bristling, she sat up straighter. "Pity doesn't pay the bills. I have no time for that, either."

"To be honest, I don't feel the least bit sorry for ye. I'm only saying it can't have been easy, burying a husband, leaving everything behind, starting over in a new town, all with a youngster to raise, yet." He took a swallow of the tea. "I'm curious, though."

She sipped her own tea, and waited for him to explain.

"Why didn't ye head back to Philadelphia when ye lost yer man, so ye could be near yer people?"

"I have no people," she said, wrapping her hands around the cup. She stared into the dark, shimmering liquid. "I heard about the accident a month before Adam was to be born. The news was such a shock that—"

"Accident? What news?"

She took a deep breath. "There was a fire in the church. Everyone inside was trapped. It was wintertime, so the windows were closed tight. They–they—"

J. J. placed his big hands atop hers and stared deep into her eyes. "So, ye're alone, too, then," he said, his voice barely above a whisper. "Now there's something I know about."

No man had touched her, not since Sean. His palms, pressing against the backs of her hands as she held the cup, were warm, and despite the calluses (or because of them?), surprisingly soothing. "I'm not totally alone. I have a grandmother."

His eyes brightened. "There, now. Why, that's wonderful. Is she here in Currituck?"

Kate shook her head. "No. She's never been to Currituck. Or North Carolina, for that matter. She went home after the fire."

J. J.'s gray eyes darkened, reminding her of the color of the sky, just before a storm. "Home?" He paused. "Not to–not to England."

Coming from him, it sounded like a foul word. "To England. Yes. How did you know?"

He released her hands, stood, and headed for the door. "Just a guess, Missus Flynn."

"If I'm to call you J. J.," she said, following him, "I'm afraid you'll have to stop calling me 'Missus Flynn.'"

He nodded. "Fair's fair, I s'pose." He opened the door.

"Thank you for the model."

" 'Twas me pleasure."

"I know Adam is going to love it." She hesitated. "Wouldn't you rather give it to him? So you can see his reaction for yourself, I mean?"

"Maybe you'll just tell me about it, next time I see ye."

And just like that, he was gone.

She brought the cups and saucers to the sink, rethinking their conversation, wondering what about it had caused him to leave so abruptly. Something to do with England, but what? And why such a negative reaction? She changed into her nightclothes and wondered about it some more. An hour after that, she was still wandering from window to window, restless, agitated, tense, though she could think of no reason to feel this way. Perhaps the view would calm her, soothe her, as it so often had.

She grabbed her thick, fringed shawl and stepped onto the porch. Well, it wasn't a porch, exactly. The balcony had been the only improvement she hadn't made with her own two hands. It had also been the only renovation she considered a necessary luxury.

Most of the time, going to the window had been a comfort to her, but there were also instances when the faint scent of soot and charred wood wafted into her nostrils, reminding her that years ago, a ferocious blaze killed the family that had lived in this house. At almost the same time in history, hundreds of miles north of Currituck, fire had killed her family, too.

If she'd known that neither scrubbing nor painting nor the passage of time would eradicate the awful odors and the images they conjured, she might not have purchased the property, because when the scents assaulted her senses, Kate could almost feel the heat of the flames, could almost hear their hiss and crackle, hungrily chomping through the house, room by room.

Time after time, when the pictures appeared, she'd throw open the window as far as it would go and pray for God Almighty to send a breeze to blow the haunting images from her memory. If anyone else noticed the essences reminiscent of the fire, they hadn't mentioned it to Kate, so she had no choice but to believe the visions were nothing but products of an overactive imagination.

Each time the eerie event enveloped her, Kate yearned for the crisp pungency of briny air, but no matter how deeply she inhaled, the clinging stench of scorched lumber would not leave her.

If only she could step outside, she'd thought, and get away from the searing memories!

But the apartment was on the second floor. She could escape the dreamlike pictures only by going by way of the steep, narrow staircase that ran through the center of the house, and that meant leaving Adam upstairs, alone and unprotected. Kate wouldn't do that, not even for the moments it would take to clear her head of the horrible scene.

That's why she'd hired Jake Carter to attach a small enclosed platform outside her window, with stairs leading to the ground.

Now, she stood looking out to sea. As the night cloaked her, Kate wondered why so many people feared the darkness. True, it was more difficult to see than in the daytime, and true, an assortment of predators stalked the shadows. But there was comfort in the thick, inky blackness, too, if one chose to see it, to feel it, the kind of serenity, born in silence, that grows stronger with each passing moment.

She likened the hours between twilight and daybreak to a warm quilt, thrown by a protective parent over a sleeping child. The dark invited calm, and quiet, and reassurance. It promised peace and contentment if one dwelt on things that were beautiful about it, rather than the fearful things that darkness could inspire.

Things like a bright canopy of stars, twinkling, glittering, shimmering like minuscule crystals. Every time she looked into the night sky, Kate was reminded her of her life-loving sister, who routinely gathered petals, or sand, or feathers and, giggling with glee, flung them skyward. Kate often wondered if, on the day the Lord had created the earth, he'd cast the spangles into the heavens in a similar way. She remembered, too, that when she was but a girl, her mother had told her the celestial bodies were God's angels, winking to assure the humans He'd assigned them to protect that all was well.

Another pleasantry of the night was the ever-changing face of the moon. Sometimes, it appeared slender as a new-trimmed fingernail, and sometimes, it looked as round as a child's rubber ball. Its lunar light beamed down upon the earth in opaque fronds. "The fingers of God's hand," her mother had said, "reaching out to give His children a reassuring pat on the head as they settle in for a long night's sleep."

For a reason she couldn't explain, Kate felt none of the

usual uplifting security tonight as she looked toward the
ebony sky. Perhaps it was the eerie wind that soughed, soft-
yet-sharp from the sea. Or maybe the crisp mid-May air dis-
couraged her much-needed peace.

A cool breeze riffled her hair. Kate shivered. If she was
cold—Adam had always been a restless sleeper. No doubt
he'd kicked his covers off. And she'd left his window open a
crack, so the chilly draft would be blowing over him. Kate
climbed back into her room through the window and tiptoed
toward his room.

Sure enough, the boy lay on his side, huddled in a knee-
hugging ball. Gently, she pulled up the coverlet she'd fash-
ioned from material scraps, and tucked it under his chin.
Every maternal chord in her sang out as she looked into his
sleeping face, and her eyes filled with awe-inspired, grateful
tears. *Oh, how blessed I am to have him in my life,* she
thought, clasping her hands under her chin. *Thank you, Lord,
for giving me Adam to love!* If she accomplished nothing else
in her years on this planet, she would have contributed something worthwhile in the form of this beautifully-formed child.

Kate knelt beside his bed and, carefully, so as not to wake
him, combed her fingers through his soft, cinnamony curls. A
shaft of moonlight sliced through the small opening in his
curtains, slid across the floor, up onto his bed, and illuminated
his sweet, sleeping face.

Long, dusky lashes rested on his freckled cheeks, and one
corner of his mouth turned up in the beginnings of an innocent, little-boy smile. *What are you dreaming, little one?* Kate
wondered. *Are you chasing a bullfrog? Or kicking a ball? Or
surf fishing?*

He'd tucked one small hand beneath his cheek; the other
clutched his feather pillow tight to his chest. *How can you
look so much like your father, and be nothing like him in any
other way?* A dreaded thought reverberated in her heart like
a Chinese gong: *What if he is like Sean in other ways, but*

simply isn't old enough to show it yet?

One day, the freckles peppering the bridge of his nose would fade. Would his innocence fade, too? Soon, his narrow chest would broaden and thicken with mighty muscles. Would a caring heart continue to beat inside it? Now, his long-fingered, gentle hands insisted upon using cheese for bait ("I can't stick a hook through the worms, Ma; it would hurt 'em!"). Would those same hands clench into angry fists, and cause deliberate pain someday?

He was satisfied now, happy even, with a roof over his head, enough food for his belly, a modest wardrobe, a few treasured toys. Would a never-ending yearning for more, always more, drive him to a violent end?

She pictured Sean as she'd last seen him: Slumped over the green felt poker table, dagger in one hand, dollars in the other, bleeding from a bullet hole in his temple, eyes open but unseeing.

"Not that for my only boy, Lord," she prayed, shutting her eyes tight to blot the image from her mind, "please, not that."

The boy stirred, and regretfully, Kate drew back her hand. But she continued to kneel beside him, her hands folded as in prayer. Unmindful of the hard board floor, the nip in the air, the late hour, she watched him sleep. When Adam was but a babe-in-arms, Kate spent hour after hour this way, convinced if she hadn't needed a few hours' respite herself, she could have whiled her life away, content to count his breaths, his tiny murmurs, his sweet sighs.

I know that his body will grow, Lord, his mind will broaden and his feet may well carry him far from home. I know these things are part of Your greater plan for Adam, but won't You let it happen slowly, please? Let him linger awhile as a boy, Lord, before that headlong rush into manhood.

Regardless of the timing God attached to Adam's life, Kate was not the kind of mother who would try to forestall those things, not even if, when he became a man, something—a job, a woman, a burning desire to see the world—might take him from Currituck. Someday, she would give her full-grown son this advice: "If you can remember only one commandment, make it the Golden Rule, for it will guide you in every area of your life."

Maybe you shouldn't wait until he's a man to give him that advice, Kate told herself. *Maybe you should teach it to him now. Maybe you should have told him about it long ago.*

Before meeting up with Bobby and his gang, Adam had been a happy, cooperative child who needed rare reminders to do his chores, an occasional prompt to do his homework. The only orders he obeyed since his association with the ruffians came directly from Bobby, leader of the pack.

But lately—

Lately, he was doing his chores without being cued. And every job, no matter how menial or unpleasant, was done as though he were aiming for perfection. Most of the time, Kate happily admitted, he hit the bull's eye, and even on the rare occurrence when he missed, she could see proof of his good intentions on his face, in his stance, and that evidence was there from the moment he climbed out of bed in the morning 'til he closed his eyes again at night.

Her sweet, thoughtful boy was back, and Kate knew there could only be one explanation for the sudden transformation: J. J. O'Keefe.

Kate stood and pressed a light, loving kiss to Adam's temple. "Sleep well, sweet boy, and may the angels bless your dreams."

And as she climbed into her own bed, Kate smiled. "And may the angels bless your dreams as well, J. J. O'Keefe."

He'd earned sweet dreams, after all, for having given her back her boy.

❧

J. J. didn't understand the feelings warring inside him, because living by his motto should have been simple and straightforward: "Avoid all things English."

They'd cost him everything, after all—his parents and siblings, his home, his Ireland. One by one, they'd succumbed to the famine and its after-effects. Some slipped quietly, slowly away, the anguished victims of starvation; the rest had gone quickly amid the haunting wails of fever-induced pain.

One by one, he'd buried them. And when the last of them was laid to rest in the cold, damp ground, he stood alone in the rocky hillside overlooking Galway Bay and bid them a last farewell.

Why he had not been taken, J. J. didn't know. Why had he been the only O'Keefe God had spared? Was it so he could become a harbinger, one of the few remaining who could remember and record the atrocities?

The horrors were too excessive to number. The English deserved to be feared, had earned the hatred of his people. But because they'd stolen, starved, and beaten the fight out of the Irish, those with any fight left in them sought ways to escape. J. J. had been one of those.

They had taken everyone, everything, and continued cutting a wide and destructive swath over the land. J. J. might have survived there, even alone, if he'd O'Keefe land to farm, if he'd had his father's blacksmith shop to run, if they'd left him his own carpentry tools. It broke his heart to see the same thing happening to friends and neighbors. There was nothing he could do to stop it.

But he couldn't stay and watch the persistent ruination of his beloved Ireland, either.

He'd said a final prayer over their graves, because if his plan succeeded, he would not be back to pray over them again.

That very night, when the moon slipped behind a cloud, he crept aboard a ship bound for New York's harbor. For weeks, he hid in the bowels of the boat as the ocean's heaving, swelling waves jostled his weary, lonely body. Only when the sun was swallowed up by the horizon, and the world grew grim with gloom, did he dare sneak from his hideaway, crawling in the shadows like the shipboard roaches and rats that shared his space, in search of scraps of food and drops to drink.

Thoughts of New York kept him alive. There was no denying that America had promised freedom to thousands of his countrymen, but liberty was not what had lured J. J. to its hallowed shores. The Yanks had fought long and hard against British oppression, and they'd won. He needed no more information than that to know he would feel at home there.

Provided he could make it there.

If the swabbies or their captain found him, he'd be thrown overboard. He'd heard stories of stowaways who'd treaded water for days before exhaustion—or hungry sharks—overtook them. And if he didn't succumb to some dreaded disease from the flea bites he'd endured, sleeping among the rats, maybe the tainted water or the spoiled food would do him in. Better any one of those ends, he believed, were more fair and equitable than what the English had done to the Irish.

As a boy, he'd had a healthy fear of death. Healthy, because it had prevented him taking foolish chances, like shortcuts across the peat bogs, or seeing how near the edge of a cliff he could stand without falling into the bay—or sneaking into old man McPhereson's store to steal a cake or cookies.

As a young man, he'd feared it because he'd learned to appreciated what life could offer, the friendship of a father, the kinship of a brother, the love of a good wife, the birth of a child.

Huddled among the sacks and crates and boxes in the foul-smelling hold of that ship, J. J. had no fear of death. He had but one fear: That he wouldn't make it to the green fields of Americay. But he'd made it, thank God, he'd made it!

Now, he lay in his bunk, above the business he'd fought for and built with his own two hands, a free man, a North Carolinian, an American! Smiling, J. J. clasped his hands behind his head, staring at the rafters. Shimmering moonlight squeaked between the boards above and glinted from the nail-tips that protruded through the underside of the rough-hewn lumber-and-shingle roof.

Kate's eyes gleam like that, he thought, half smiling.

And then he remembered she was half English, and his smile faded.

Ye can't fault her for that; she had no say in who her ancestors were.

If English blood flowed in her veins, she couldn't be as good and decent as she seemed to be.

Could she?

He wanted to believe that she could, because in moments like these, when he was alone with nothing but his own thoughts, he liked to pretend that a normal future was possible for him, after all, that love and family and life could be his again, beside a woman like Kate Flynn.

Kate O'Keefe.

It sounded right. Sounded good. Sounded like something Danny Flannigan down at Kerry's Pub might put to music if the fever hadn't sent the Dark Fairy to take the fiddler, too. J. J. sat up with a start, punched the mattress, and cursed the English. *How can ye even be thinkin' of linkin' yer life to an Englishwoman? Especially so soon after layin' eyes on her!*

He could be thinking it, because in her soft brown eyes, he saw all the misery and loneliness of her soul. Oh, she put on a good front, to be sure—for her boy's sake, no doubt—with her happy face and her lilting voice. But the sadness was there, nonetheless, just beneath the surface.

And it was there because she'd made the sorry mistake of marrying an Irishman, of all things! That one of his own could raise a hand to a woman boggled J. J.'s mind. How Sean Flynn could harm a lass as lovely and loving as Kate. . .

Surely she was loving. Could she be anything else, when she'd only agreed to marry Sean Flynn to keep her parents' business from going belly-up?

She was a scrappy little thing. If anyone needed proof, he need only cite the day he'd overheard her, defending the Indian woman on the steps of the feed and grain. He'd been across the street in the bank when voices, raised in anger, caught his attention. He'd stood in the open doorway, watching, listening, amazed that someone her size would take on two full-grown men and a woman twice her weight on behalf of the Algonquin princess.

He'd seen Running Deer before, many times, pacing up and down Currituck's shore. "Stay away from that one," Abe Peters had warned. "Her own people won't have nothin' to do with her; they say she's crazy as a bedbug." Shaking his head, Abe had added, "The In'di'ns threwed her out of the village, way I hear it. And she's been livin' in a cave over yonder ever since."

"Why do they think she's crazy?"

"Seems she found a map once't, hammered into leather by the ancients. The missionary what taught her to read helped her decipher it. It was more a tall tale, if'n you ask me, 'cause it were a picture on it of the Sound twice the size it is now." He scratched his bristly chin. "I tolt her there had to be a mistake. 'Mebbe the mapmaker was drunk when he drawed that picture,' I tolt her. 'Mebbe he was old and feeble, and his eyesight was a-failin' him when he made the sketch.'

"But she weren't havin' none of it. She b'lieved ever' last word of it. Said we'd all best be more careful 'bout how we treat them trees, 'cause if we didn't take care, one day, they'd all be gone."

"What trees?" J. J. had wanted to know.

He pointed a gnarled finger. "Why, them cedars over yonder, a-course. According to Running Deer, a hunnert years from now, there won't be nothin' left of 'em but a couple o' scraggly poles stickin' up outta the water."

J. J. chuckled. "It'll take folks a lot more'n a hundred years to use up that much lumber."

"You ain't followin' me, Irish," Abe said, shaking his white-haired head. "People ain't gonna be the end o' them cedars, the ocean will!"

Frowning, J. J. shook his head.

"I'm tellin' you," Abe warned, walking away, "watch out for that'n. She's crazy as a bedbug," he tossed over his shoulder. "Crazy as a bedbug."

Much as J. J. hated to admit it, the story had sent a chill up his spine.

But Kate hadn't feared the Indian woman. He admired her more than he cared to admit.

Half English or not, she was the best thing that had happened to him in a long, long time.

four

"I can't believe ye talked me into this, Thaddius."

"Let's get one thing straight right up front, son: Nobody talks J. J. O'Keefe into anything, least of all a feeble old man like me."

J. J. grinned. "And the only thing feeble about you, Thaddius Crofton," he countered, "is yer reasons for askin' me here."

Thaddius lifted his shoulders in an innocent shrug. "It's a Sunday social, nothin' more. The pastor encourages us to—"

"Gather the flock?"

"Say what you will, O'Keefe; you're as glad to be here as I am to have you here."

It was J. J.'s turn to shrug. "Fried chicken and a slice of Mary's apple pie is why I'm glad to be here."

"Well, you know better'n most that nothin' comes free in this life. Consider the preacher's sermon payment for your free meal."

J. J. planted both boots flat on the floor and crossed his arms over his chest just as Mary leaned forward. "Will the two of you stop with your whispering?" she scolded sweetly, pressing a gloved hand to her husband's knee. "I can't hear a word Pastor Hall is saying!"

"Sorry, Mother," said Thaddius from the corner of his mouth. "I was just tellin' J. J. here that—"

"I heard what you were tellin' J. J." She flashed him a loving look, a mischievous smile, and rolled her eyes. "The whole congregation likely heard what you were tellin' J. J. Now for heaven's sake, dear, will the both of you hush, so I can hear the message?"

Thaddius gave her hand a gentle squeeze. "Sorry, Mother," he said again.

J. J. stared straight ahead and fought the feelings of jealousy, swirling in his gut.

He'd never envied a man in all his life.

He'd known his share of wealthy men, and those with the power to influence. There were great orators and Harvard-educated teachers. Some were bigger, stronger, even, than J. J. himself, and their prowess had brought them glory or fame, or both. A few got by on little more than their good looks.

But whether these men came by their good fortune by the sweat of their brows or a kiss from Lady Luck, J. J. didn't begrudge them what they had, nor did he wish to have the same, because he knew full well that time would slowly erase the things they were so proud of on this earth, physical appearance, intelligence, material possessions, the accolades of their peers. And as for money, well, if the English hadn't taught him that a man could be rich and powerful one day, poor and helpless the next, then he was a man who simply could not be taught! Those things had their place, but they went hand in hand with qualities more enduring. Qualities like generosity and bravery.

No, he couldn't think of a single reason why he'd want to envy another.

But he knew why he envied Thaddius Crofton.

Thaddius had something money could not buy, something he could not have secured by wielding political power or brute force. And he would have had it regardless of whether or not he'd been graced with a perfectly sculpted physique, like Michelangelo's "David," or the body and face of Quasimoto. Thaddius had the love of a good woman, and he'd had it all his adult life.

J. J. had heard it said that a mate is chosen by the Almighty on the day a man is born. Unfortunately, the Lord didn't write the intended lady's name on a slip of paper and tuck it into the baby boy's bunting. As a result, some men spend a lifetime searching for the perfect woman and never find her. Others try them all on for size, to see if maybe this one fits, and of course none of them do. There were those who'd been kicked in the teeth by love a few times before stumbling into the arms of the real thing, and those who seemed to find it without having looked at all.

Thaddius was one of those.

If J. J. had been a guest at their wedding, he knew he would have witnessed their new, true love just as surely as he was seeing it now, after they'd been together for more than sixty years. They'd shared a bed, a home, a life, raised six strapping sons and two darling daughters. There had been hard times, but even the hard times had been good in their own way. And the proof of that was written on their faces and voices, in the gentle, loving looks and soft, sweet words.

J. J. didn't envy the old man his business; he had a thriving company of his own. Nor did he hunger for the fellow's money; there was more than enough in his own bank account to provide for his needs. He didn't wish for a home like Thaddius's, for he had perfectly comfortable living quarters. And though it was rare to see Thaddius without at least two friends buzzing about, J. J. didn't long for a wide social circle, because he'd always been a solitary sort.

Thaddius had a woman who cared about him, and that's what J. J. envied, what he wanted for himself.

He didn't yearn to have a woman who'd do for him what Mary did for Thaddius—and admittedly, she did hundreds of small personal favors every day, and Thaddius in turn looked with favor upon his beloved. J. J. now understood the expression "to curry favor with the one you love."

He was perfectly capable of taking care of himself. He'd taught himself to cook his own meals, and did a fair to middlin' job, if he did say so himself. He'd learned to sew on a button or darn a hole in his sock, and how to wash his own dirty work shirts, and he kept his sparsely-furnished apartment neat and tidy.

No, it wasn't what Mary did for Thaddius that made J. J. wish for a slice of the old man's life, it was the way she did them and the reasons that inspired her to do them in the first place.

He'd seen other wives straighten their husbands' ties. Had watched them smooth shirt collars, trudge to the green market, hang laundry, sweep the porch. They should be credited, he supposed, with "taking care of" their men. But the bored, resentful expressions on their faces told J. J. how they really felt: They saw their mates as wearying obligations, so naturally the things they did for them were viewed as hard, backbreaking work.

Oh, to be sure their men were good for something: bringing home a paycheck, hauling in the wood, smashing spiders, lifting heavy loads, and chasing off offensive stray dogs or wandering hobos. "You're so much better at the manly chores than I am," he'd heard one wife say, her voice and face feigning a "You're my hero!" look. But once he'd repaired the carriage wheel and they were on their way, the wife's face quickly resumed its "You're my millstone" expression, because she saw him, as so many wives saw their husbands, as a bother, yet another item on her already too-long list of dull and dreary chores, and nothing more.

Not so with Mary Crofton!

When Mary tidied Thaddius's tie, or smoothed his collar (or scolded him for whispering during the sermon) she looked neither bored nor bothered. Rather, she looked like a woman who was deeply in love, even after more than six decades of cooking for her man, and washing his shirts, and sweeping his porch.

Kate would be that kind of wife.

Oh, and what would he give her in return? His life, the sweat of his brow, his waking breath, his last thought before he slept.

He looked at her, sitting there on the other side of the little church with her boy at her side, staring straight ahead, smiling and nodding in response to the preacher's sermon. She was lovely, so very lovely, and no man in his right mind could argue with that, what with her shiny hair and big eyes. She had a smile that could warm the coldest night. If it was true that music could soothe the savage beast, Kate need only speak a word or two, and even the angriest tiger would be calmed.

He'd been in her home, had seen with his own two eyes the precision, the orderliness of her life, from the conversation-friendly positioning of furnishings to the colorful carpets and curtains. To the casual observer, it might appear the afghans and throw pillows had been nonchalantly placed, but J. J. was no casual observer. He could almost picture her, standing in a doorway, squinting, chewing a knuckle as she carefully chose the perfect location for each doily and knick-knack, a place that would balance scatter rugs and candlesticks and books on the shelves.

The precision of her needlework was more proof of her attention to detail. She put everything she had into everything she did. *If Kate puts that much effort into the everyday, routine things in life, imagine how she'd love her man!* J. J. thought.

If he needed evidence to back up his assessment, he needn't look any farther than the way she looked at Adam. The love shone in her eyes so powerfully bright, J. J. wondered why it didn't blind the boy!

Kate lifted her chin, then inclined her head, bringing his attention back to her face. Even in profile, a person could tell that she had eyes as wide and winsome as a doe's, with long, dark, lustrous lashes. Those eyes had been responsible for the way he'd caught himself daydreaming the other afternoon. He'd been putting the final coat of varnish on a mast when he found himself staring off into space, grinning like a fool, trying to come up with a name for the color of her eyes. Not brown, exactly, but not green or blue, either. He settled for "beautiful."

The brows above them were dark and delicately arched, like the gentle curve of a boat's prow, rising and lowering as her expressive face reflected her mood, her tone of voice, or reacted to things around her.

Her cheekbones were high and softly-rounded and pink, and he'd never seen a more perfect neck, fluting delicately down from her chin like a well-carved figurehead, long and gracefully curved and as creamy-white as the smooth, finely-pored skin of her face.

J. J. had never seen her with her hair down around her narrow, feminine shoulders. Would it feel as thick and velvety as it looked? Would it slip through his fingers like strands of satin? He imagined that hair, billowing like a wind-filled sail at sea.

Physically, she was everything a woman should be, soft and delicate and dainty, from the top of her head to the toes of her tiny feet. She had the littlest waist he'd ever seen—a man's fingers would likely meet if he wrapped them 'round her middle—which flared gently into shapely hips. Could she be anything but flawless?

The first time they'd met, she'd matched his angry glare with one of her own. Like a mama lion hovers over her cub, Kate would have fought to the death if need be to protect her son. *This is not a woman who can be trifled with,* he'd thought at the time.

There was no denying it: Kate Flynn fascinated him. Why else would he be sitting here, sweltering in this too-small, too-crowded church? He'd vowed never to pay homage to the God who had allowed such savagery to take place in his homeland, but he hadn't even thought of that when Thaddius invited him to the meeting. He'd heard that occasionally, to meet a deadline for a customer, Kate missed a Sunday service. Thaddius hadn't finished asking the question before J. J.

agreed to come, because he saw it as an opportunity to see her again.

Now, as he continued to watch her, J. J. tried to ignore the roiling in the pit of his stomach, the hard beating of his heart, the perspiration that slicked his palms, the dryness that parched his throat. *All this in reaction to merely looking at her? What's to become of ye if ever ye're lucky enough to take her in yer arms!* he wondered, half smiling.

It had been a mistake to allow himself such a thought, because it filled his being with longing. He wanted to protect and provide for her, to comfort and treasure her, to brand her his with kisses and touches and promises of everlasting fidelity.

Suddenly, she began to squirm in the pew, and with a lace-gloved hand, adjusted the bow of her bonnet, the folds of her skirt, the buttons of her bodice. And with no warning whatsoever, turned her lovely wide-eyed face toward him and looked straight into his eyes.

For an instant, they sat, bound one to the other by an invisible thread of yearning.

Just like that early-May evening when, as he'd walked alone on the dock, he'd gotten that mysterious "Somebody's watching me" feeling. It had awakened an incredible urge to look up, and when he did, he'd seen her, there in her window, elbows resting on the sill and a cheek in a palm, her big-eyed gaze locked on him. The connection had lasted, had held them for a heartbeat, maybe two, before her eyes widened and her hands fluttered near her throat and she disappeared into the shadows of her room.

Though he looked hard for it, J. J. couldn't see the barest hint of a smile, couldn't find a glint of the teasing humor that had glowed in her eyes the night he'd dropped by her place with the model boat.

It was said that the eyes were the windows to the soul. If that were true, she was looking straight into his soul, taking his measure as a man. He didn't know if he wanted her reading him that way; what would she think of all the hard feelings and hatred written on his heart?

So he grabbed a hymnal from the wooden pocket attached to the pew in front of him, opened it, and pretended to be engrossed in the notes on the near-transparent pages.

❧

Kate, for her part, had been feeling for quite some time that perhaps someone was watching her. Never would she have guessed it might be J. J. O'Keefe!

To her knowledge, he hadn't attended services since moving to Currituck. At least, she'd never seen him in church, and she'd only missed a handful of Sundays since making the coastal town her home. Quite frankly, the fact that he was here at all stunned her almost as much as catching him looking at her.

But why was he studying her so intently? And what was the expression, burning in his eyes? Kate's heart turned over as something intense flared inside her.

She blinked, fighting the bewilderment swirling in her head. He was looking at her in exactly that same way as he had when he'd seen her at the window, that evening several weeks ago, a deep, determined stare filled with whispered expectation.

But expectation of what?

As if hypnotized she sat, mesmerized by his presence. Just what did he want from her? she wondered with somber curiosity. The question hammered at her until his almost-innocent expression darkened, as if he were drawing himself in, which, as it turned out, was exactly what he'd been doing, she realized. Immediately, she regretted the change in him, and blinking, Kate pressed her fingertips to her lips as his brow furrowed, as his mouth tightened, as he looked away.

Kate was astonished at the sense of disappointment she felt. They had shared something special, something meaningful for however brief a time, and he'd ended it, quite consciously and deliberately.

Why did her heart ache so? Why did she miss him, as if he'd left her to take a long, solitary journey?

Except for those two precious occasions when their eyes had met, Kate and J. J. hadn't shared anything more than idle conversation. So why did she feel this sense of longing, and loss, and sadness?

He'd been friendly when he'd stopped by to deliver the model boat for Adam, and their conversation had been so warm. Had she been mistaken to think he liked her—not merely as neighbors, as fellow Currituckers—but the way a man likes a woman?

Kate sighed and loosened the bow of her bonnet. *Must be too tight, and it's cutting off the blood supply to your brain,* she told herself, frowning slightly. *Stop behaving like an addle-brained twit, like a school girl in the throes of her first crush. You're in the House of the Lord, for heaven's sake!*

She couldn't remember a time when she'd allowed anything to interfere with her time to worship. Whether home alone, saying her daily devotions, or here with fellow parishioners, sharing prayers, she had never let the everyday frustrations of life keep her from focusing on Him.

What's wrong with you? Kate demanded of herself. *Why are you behaving like a wanton hussy!*

Shamefaced, Kate felt the heat of a blush creep into her cheeks and stared guiltily into her lap.

She was behaving this way, she admitted, because despite her vow, she was beginning to feel something for J. J. O'Keefe. Beginning to feel? Why, she'd felt it from the moment they'd met! Right from the start, she'd sensed something special, something decent in this man. She'd hesitated to admit it, even in the privacy of her mind, because she was afraid, so very afraid, of making another horrendous mistake. The vow she'd made, after all, had been simple and straightforward: *Never again commit yourself to a man who hasn't committed himself to God.*

Sean had not been a believer, and J. J. was not a church-goer. Was that the same thing? Though Sean had come to America with his parents before his first birthday, he'd been born in Dublin. And J. J. had lived all but the past few years on the wild and rugged Burren, near Galway Bay. If his past was any barometer, he had no measurable Christianity in him. And was it any surprise?

She had tried to talk herself out of the sweet, warm feelings that rippled in her heart at thoughts of him by telling herself that surely he was worse, far worse than Sean. Because while her husband had used his fists to beat strangers into submission, he'd done it only when drink dulled his wits. J. J., on the other hand, had stepped consciously and deliberately into the ring, hundreds of times, willing to face any opponent who thought himself strong enough to beat "The Annihilator." According to Thaddius, J. J. never lost a match, a fact that enabled him to line his pockets with the winnings, money gambled away by hard-working men from New York to North Carolina.

Without realizing it, she'd established a pattern. Whenever she had a positive thought about him, she'd counter it with a negative one. When she saw him using his brawn to help Mary and Thaddius unload the heavy shipments that arrived weekly at their store, she drew a mental picture of him using that same brawn to pound the faces of less powerful men into bloody pulp. When she acknowledged the artistry of the hands that had turned raw wood into beautiful sailing vessels, she painted a mental scene of those same hands, rendering his competitors unconscious. When she saw the results of the time he'd spent with her son, teaching Adam to make good use of his idle time, she consciously considered how J. J. had once made use of his.

Trouble was, the see-sawing evidence wasn't building the case she'd hoped it would, because no matter how hard she tried, the good always outweighed the bad. But which was he, good and decent as she'd first suspected? Or mean and evil, as proved by his past? And if violence had once been his driving force, had he turned over a new leaf? Or was his peaceable nature merely a facade? Kate wanted—no, needed—to find the answers to these questions, because how could she pin her hopes and dreams to a future with him without those answers?

The trouble with that man, Kate fussed inwardly, *is that he's too complicated. Just when I think I've figured him out, he goes and does something to confuse me!*

The congregation stood in unison, pulled out their hymnals and turned, as instructed, to "Amazing Grace." As the strains of the organ swelled and the voices of parishioners rose, Kate mouthed the words. "How sweet the sound, that saved a wretch like me."

But her mind was not on the music, nor on the lovely lyrics. Like that of an unruly child, it wandered hither and yon, from J. J.'s handsome face to his resonant, masculine voice, to his diamond-bright gray eyes.

His eyes.

They'd widened, then narrowed when she turned and found him staring at her, but not so much that she couldn't read the surprised discomfort in them.

A small smile curved her lips.

Because his startled, embarrassed expression was proof that now he knew exactly how it felt to be caught.

❧

It was hot and steamy, even before the sun came up, but if the citizens of this tiny coastal city noticed, it didn't stop them from celebrating in full regalia. For weeks, while the town's housewives were busy sewing the banners that now flapped brightly on every storefront, the men were erecting a multi-tiered gazebo in the center of town to get ready for the Fourth of July festivities.

The big day was here at last, and the hard-working volunteers weren't about to let a little heat and humidity stop them from enjoying it to its fullest.

Wooden tables stood in a U-formation under the pines. On the right-hand of the U, dozens of pies and cakes and mountains of cookies kept the sultry breezes from lifting the tablecloths into the air like small, red-and-white sails. In the center section, fried chicken, roasted pork, and spit-charred beef had been arranged on huge serving platters. And on the left, breads and rolls of every shape and variety sat in piles amid the tableware.

The day before, Currituck children had shoveled dirt into the road ruts and covered the entire length of Main Street with sawdust to keep the dust at a minimum.

All dressed up in her red, white, and blue finery, Currituck, North Carolina, was ready to celebrate America's seventy-ninth birthday.

At the stroke of nine, there would be a parade. Later, the band would gather in the shady bandstand to play an assortment of toe-tapping tunes, their brass horns and silver flutes gleaming in the sunlight.

There would be a two-legged race, a pie-eating contest, and a muscleman competition. The children had insisted on a dunking booth, and their fathers had insisted on a kissing booth. Ladies and gentlemen who had not yet joined hands in the holy sacrament of marriage were eligible to participate in the boxed lunch auction.

And wearing their Sunday finest, the fine people of Currituck greeted one another by tipping the white straw hats perched on heads, big and small, old and young, male and female alike.

Kate hadn't seen J. J. since that Sunday two weeks ago, when he'd hot-footed it out of the church at the end of the sermon, foregoing the usual after service hand-shaking and well-wishes, and the potluck supper that followed as well. Mary had cross-examined Thaddius about the Irishman's absence. But the elderly gent refused any comment other than "J. J. is a grown man; I guess he knows if he wants a chicken dinner or not."

She found it hard to believe he'd come to church for no reason other than the free meal, because if the food had been the explanation for his attendance, would their casual exchange have been reason enough to leave without it?

Only if he wasn't the rough-and-tumble man he pretended to be. Or if he had a shy, awkward side that didn't show in his day-to-day dealings with fellow Currituckers.

She'd caught him gawking as surely as he'd caught her that day in May, and just as she'd retreated into the shadows the moment she'd been found out, he'd high-tailed it back to his warehouse without so much as a howdy-do at the conclusion of the meeting.

It was a side of him she hadn't known existed—a side of him that plucked every womanly chord in her.

She hadn't seen him since, not in or near his warehouse, not walking on the dock, not ducking into the Crofton's feed and grain store. But surely he'd show up at the town's annual gala. At least, she hoped he would, so she could try and make it up to him for witnessing his awkwardness.

In the event that he did show up, Kate chose her outfit carefully. Patched together from scraps of cotton she'd used to make the Chandler twins' matching dresses, and leftovers from a bolt of bright white, Kate had made a narrow-skirted gown with a boat-neck bodice and three-quarter length sleeves. She'd used the red for the outer pleats, and the white for the inner ones, so that the only times the ivory showed was when she moved and separated the pleats. She'd trimmed the sweeping, scooped neckline and cuffs with tiny, tight-pressed pleats. And in honor of the day, she'd borrowed a narrow blue belt from her favorite skirt.

Kate believed in balance in all things, and to offset her black high-button boots, she wore a black cord around her neck and tied it in a minuscule bow at her throat.

Without exception, she wound her hair into a sensible bun every morning. She had never particularly liked the style, thinking it looked like a monkey grinder's hat without the stripes. But it did the job of keeping tendrils from escaping and getting in her way as she worked, and so she piled it atop her head every morning, and secured it with two large hairpins. Today, because it was a special occasion, she'd gathered the hair from the crown forward into a loose braid, and wound red, white, and blue satin ribbons through it.

She'd baked a pan of apple cobbler, and covered it with a blue and white flowered tea towel. She was positioning it among the other tasty treats when she heard footsteps shooshing across the lawn behind her. *Adam, no doubt,* she thought, grinning, *come to see if he can sneak a fingerful of fudge icing from Mary's cake, or a cookie from the schoolmarm's plate.* She opened her mouth to tell him to wait until everyone else had been invited to the table.

"Looks good enough to eat."

She'd have recognized that rich baritone anywhere. Kate pretended the desserts needed more rearranging. "Mr. O'Keefe," she said, "I'm so glad you decided to join us today."

"Haven't missed a Currituck July Fourth since I settled here. Why would I start now?"

"That's strange. Neither have I. You'd think we would have bumped into one another, wouldn't you?"

She felt a warm, heavy hand upon her shoulder, guiding her to turn around. "That's quite a dress ye're wearin' there, Mrs. Flynn. Ye made it yerself, I presume?"

His eyes glittered in the sunlight like shards of gleaming glass, and he tilted his head, awaiting her answer. Her heart was beating so hard and fast, she worried he might be able to see it thumping, right through her skin. Kate pressed a palm to her chest, just in case. "Yes," she said, "I made it from scraps."

His brows flickered with confusion. "Scraps? Whatever d'ye mean?"

She gave a little shrug. "You know, the pieces I cut from the bolts, pieces I didn't need for the dresses. Seems a shame to let all that good material go to waste, so I always try to make something from them."

A muscle quivered in his jaw before he eased into a smile that started her pulse racing.

"Man has to admire a woman who's not wasteful."

As he spoke, his gaze slid over her features so slowly, it was as though she could feel it, caressing her forehead, pressing against her cheek, stroking her throat.

Then their eyes locked, his flashing with curiosity, hers rounded with amazement at the lazy seductiveness she saw on his face.

"This is becomin' a habit, Mrs. Flynn."

Kate blinked. "This? I—ah—What's becoming a habit, Mr. O'Keefe?"

J. J.'s quiet chuckle rumbled from him like the low warning growl of a panther. "This starin' into one another's eyes, that's what. I'm afraid if we keep it up, we'll get folks' tongues to waggin' for sure."

But even as he said it, she noticed his hand continued to rest upon her shoulder. "Forgive me for saying so, Mr. O'Keefe, but your eyes are such an unusual color. I've seen shades of blue and green and brown, but I've never seen any the color of the sky before a storm." Pursing her lips in a teasing smile, she added, "That's my excuse. What's yours?"

"Don't need one," he said without hesitation. "If anyone should ask what all the oglin' is about, I'll simply tell 'em the truth."

Her heart skipped a beat. "And what might that be?"

J. J. took half a step closer and put his free hand on her other shoulder. His brows dipped low in the center of his forehead as he took a deep breath. "That I may as well look.

It does me no good to close me eyes 'cause ye're still there."

The sweetness of his words took her breath away.

She felt his warm breath fanning her face when he whispered, "Ah, but ye're a vision, Mrs. Flynn, the sort who inspires men to write poetry."

Kate held her breath, searched his face for a sign—even the smallest one—that he might be toying with her. If she saw so much as a trace or a flicker of teasing, it would be her turn to run like a frightened rabbit, as he had last Sunday after church. But she found his scrutiny unwavering, saw no hint of taunting there, and breathed a sigh of relief.

"I seem to recall," she began in a slow, soft voice, "that we agreed not to refer to one another by our surnames, Mr. O'Keefe."

His left brow lifted in puzzlement.

She glanced at each of his hands, firmly attached to her shoulders, and with her own free hand, gestured at the mere inches that separated them. "Here we stand for God and all His angels to see, and the whole town as well." She shrugged one shoulder. " 'Mrs. Flynn' and 'Mr. O'Keefe' seem awfully formal under the circumstances, don't you agree?"

For an instant, J. J. continued to stare into her eyes. Gradually, faint laugh lines began to crinkle at the outer corners of his eyes, and he leaned closer, closer still, until he could rest his chin atop her head. "I'd be a lot more agreeable if—"

He leaned back far enough to look into her eyes again.

"If what?"

"Well," he said, winking, tucking in a corner of his mouth, "whenever I strike a bargain, I like to do something to make it stick."

Kate smiled. "Of course. Like a handshake, you mean?"

He looked off toward the church, where folks were beginning to gather for the parade, and nodded, J. J. pursed his lips. "That would work, but—"

His gaze slid back to Kate's face, locked on her eyes once

more. "But I had something a little more, ah, personal in mind."

"A signature?" She laughed. "You want us to sign a document to—"

It dawned on her suddenly where he was headed with his suggestion. He meant to seal their deal with a kiss!

Kate's heart thundered and her eyes widened as his face loomed closer. Instinctively, she closed her eyes. So did he.

Kate held her breath, and waited.

She thought his lips would never touch hers, but when they did, it was as though the heavens had opened up, and all the angels had begun singing, and musicians had begun playing, and dancers had begun dancing. Oh, how glorious it felt, being surrounded by his powerful arms, feeling his heart beating hard against her chest. The only man who had ever touched his lips to hers had been Sean, and there had never been anything remotely pleasant about that!

J. J.'s lips caused Kate's heart to begin beating like a war drum, caused her mind to provide harmony to the beautiful, beautiful music playing in her head.

And wasn't it fitting and proper to have music at a time like this, to brand this oh-so-special moment to her brain? She should have felt womanly long before this; she'd been married, had conceived and borne a child, after all. And yet, here and now, in this man's arms, she felt for the first time, whole and complete. Oh, what a glorious feeling it was!

The tittering of several young ladies captured their attention. Her heart ached when he lifted his head, when he took away his kiss, and stepped back slightly. Hands still on her shoulders, he wiggled his eyebrows. "I've a feelin' we've set folks' tongues to waggin'."

Smiling, Kate bit her lower lip, trying to ignore the giggling, huddling teen-aged girls who hid mischievous grins behind dainty hands.

"Um, Kate?"

She met Mary's youngest daughter's eyes. "Yes, Annie."

"Would you make me a dress like that?"

"It's nothing but scraps of—"

" 'Cause if it'll get Hank Bennett to kiss me like that, it's worth whatever price tag you tie to its sleeve!"

Resting her forehead on his chest, Kate whispered, "Next time you issue me a warning, I promise to heed it."

He lifted her chin on a bent forefinger and shrugged. Oblivious to the three young women who giggled nearby, he said, "Well, if it's all the same to you, I'd just as soon ye continue to ignore me." He wiggled his brows again. " 'Cause if ye want the truth, I rather like the outcome."

ða

"Is it true, Ma? Did he–did he kiss you?"

Kate gasped. "Adam! Wherever did you hear such a thing?"

The boy rolled his eyes. "Everybody is talking about it." He leaned closer, and nodding toward the church, whispered, "Even Pastor Hall knows."

And to think I shared my whole life's story with Mary a few months ago to keep people from talking! She hid behind her hands. "Dear Lord in heaven."

Adam slapped a hand to his forehead. "Oh, no," he groaned, "it's true, isn't it?"

Phoebe Greene darted up and gave Adam a playful shove.

"Cut it out," he barked.

"Hi, Mrs. Flynn," she sing-songed. "Adam's mad at me 'cause I saw you and Mr. O'Keefe kissing."

He rolled his eyes.

"Did you hate it, Mrs. Flynn?"

Kate came out of hiding. *Hate it? Hardly!* she thought, smiling.

"You know. The beard. The mustache." She giggled. "Did it–did it tickle?"

Kate pressed her fingertips to her temples. "I–I can't say that I noticed, Phoebe."

Adam breathed a heavy sigh. "I think I hear your mother calling, Phoebe."

She put her hands on her hips. "No you didn't," she snapped, blonde braids flopping as she shook her head. Just that quick, she turned back to Kate. "Was it really, really awful?" And before Kate could answer, she leaned forward. "Did it hurt?" she whispered.

Kate sat beside the girl, slipped an arm around her narrow shoulders. "Phoebe, honey, every night, after your father listens to your bedtime prayers, does he kiss you good-night."

Phoebe nodded.

"Does it hurt?"

Her brows rose as she gave the question a moment of serious consideration. "No."

"Is it 'really, really awful'?"

She grinned. "No, but then, he doesn't have a beard."

"Like your ma does, you mean?" Adam put in.

Kate gave him a stern glance. "Adam. Say you're sorry."

He said it, but with a pout. "Sorry."

Phoebe smiled. "What would we do for a good laugh without you, Adam?"

Wiggling his brows, he smirked. "Maybe you could get Mr. O'Keefe to tickle you with his beard."

A high-pitched voice in the distance called, "Phoebe!"

"Goodness," the little girl said, jumping up. "My mother is calling me!"

"Told ya," Adam said, bobbing his head.

The eyebrow wiggling, the mischievous grin. Instead of reminding her of Sean, Adam put her in mind of J. J.! "Adam, can I ask you a question?"

"You know the rule," he said, quoting her, "any question, any time."

Kate smiled fondly. "What do you think of. . .um. . .How do you feel about Mr. O'Keefe?"

Kate believed she already knew the answer to that, because

it had only taken a few short hours of working in the warehouse to satisfy O'Keefe's demands and yet the boy returned nearly every day, and spent every moment he could spare with the Irishman.

Still, it would be good to hear it from Adam.

He shrugged. "Oh, I dunno. He's all right I guess."

"All right? But I thought you liked him; you seem to like being around him all the time."

"It isn't him, Ma," Adam insisted, "it's what he does. I like watchin' him work. I like bein' around the boats, seein' him use all those tools."

He clearly admired J. J., and Kate suspected it had much more to do with the kind of man he was than how he earned his living. Adam couldn't admit it, of course, because he considered himself to be the man of the family. She kept her opinion to herself. At least Adam didn't dislike the man. And that might prove to be important, if—

She couldn't think about that right now.

Kate fished a few pennies from her purse. "Why don't you see if you can dunk Mr. Fisher?"

A prankish grin lit up his face. "Maybe I should try the kissing booth instead, see what all the fuss and bother is about."

Kate called his bluff. Smiling, she said, "I'm sure Miss Henderson would love that. She told me not ten minutes ago that it was her turn to. . ."

The boy wrapped both hands around his throat, as if the very idea was enough to choke the life out of him. "But–but she's the teacher!" he said, grimacing. "What's she doing in the kissing booth?"

"Same thing you're planning to do, I imagine," she replied, calm as you please, "trying to see what all the fuss and bother is about."

Adam scrambled to his feet. "Yeah, well," he began, dusting grit and grass from his knees and the seat of his pants, "maybe I'll just wait a few years. Maybe by then, Miss Henderson will be married, and her husband won't allow her to sit in the kissing booth!"

She smiled lovingly. "I'm all in favor of your waiting a few years, son, because I'm not in any hurry for you to grow up. Not in any hurry for that to happen at all."

He pocketed the coins she'd handed him and, looking around to make sure no one would see him, pressed a quick kiss to his mother's cheek. "Thanks, Ma."

She wanted to take him in her arms, hold him tight, and tell him that she loved him, too. But Kate understood how a thing like that would embarrass him if it were witnessed by the other boys. "Run along, now," she said, waving him away, "before Mr. Fisher gets so waterlogged that dunking him won't be any fun."

He raced across the lawn, yelling, "That's the booth I'm gonna volunteer for next year. It's the only place in town that's cool!"

Long after he'd gone, Kate was still sitting alone in the shade of the pines, counting all the good things in her life. She and Adam had been blessed with excellent health. They had a good, solid home, and, thanks to her thriving business, enough money for food and clothes. She'd come a long way, from Philadelphia to Raleigh, from Raleigh to Currituck.

She closed her eyes and breathed a deep, grateful sigh. *If only Ma and Pa, and Susan and George were here,* she thought, smiling slightly, *my life would be perfect.*

❧

He was about to tell her he was sorry if his kiss embarrassed her when Adam darted in as if from nowhere. J. J. stayed back; the boy was eight, his attention span as short as any other eight year old's.

J. J. need only bide his time.

He made himself comfortable by leaning against the bark of an ancient pine. *Five minutes, ten at the most,* he told himself, *and Adam will be off and runnin' in another direction.*

He couldn't believe his ears when he heard Phoebe ask about the kiss. Everybody knew she was the daughter of Currituck's biggest gossip. Once she got wind of it.

Still, every muscle in him tensed as he waited for Kate to respond. Unfortunately, she answered the girl's question with a question, making him wonder if maybe she wasn't a wee bit Irish.

"Was it really, really awful?" Phoebe asked. And J. J. hoped she would say, "Of course it wasn't. It was wonderful. Beautiful. The most magnificent. . ."

But then, he couldn't expect her to speak the words in his heart, could he?

She hadn't said what he wanted to hear. But the things she did say had made J. J. feel as good as if she had. He could almost picture her, perched on the edge of Adam's bed, combing slender, delicate fingers through his hair, eyes closed as she listened to his prayers. Admittedly, it was a bittersweet picture, because J. J. had always wanted a house full of children, who'd throw their arms around him when he came home after a long, hard day. If he could ever make that dream come true, it would be with a woman like Kate.

Adam scampered off to spend his pennies, and Kate sat back, eyes closed, a sweet, dreamy smile smoothing the worry that had creased her forehead. *What's goin' through that pretty head of yours?* he wondered. *Are ye dreamin' of more just like Adam, runnin' through our house?*

Our house? Are ye daft, man?

He realized he'd closed his eyes, too. And when he opened them, Kate was gone.

Out of sight, he told himself, *but not out of mind.*

For the truth was, she'd been on his mind every spare moment since their first official meeting that day in her dress shop.

❧

"*Psst!* Adam!"

He looked around for whoever had whispered his name.

"Adam! Psst! Over here."

He spotted Bobby, crouching in the underbrush. "What're you doin' in there? Don't you know there's—"

"Shhh!" Bobby insisted. "Get on in here, I have somethin' to tell you."

Adam wedged into the small space between the trees and the thicket. Frowning, he said, "It's cooler out there."

Bobby waved his suggestion away. "I was at the warehouse this morning."

The frown intensified. "Why?"

"No reason. Just foolin' around." He snickered. "I figured out a way for you to get even with that big dumb Irishman."

Adam's eyes narrowed. *Look who's callin' who dumb!* he thought. "Why would I want to get even with—"

Bobby grabbed his sleeve, pulled him into the underbrush beside him. "He made you work for him, that's why. Got you in trouble with your ma!"

"What's wrong with that? I did steal his lunch bucket, after all."

Bobby sneered, his nose inches from Adam's. "What's the matter, Adam? Are you a baby? Are you too yeller to get even?"

Adam hung his head. The only thing he was afraid of was being seen as a coward by Bobby and his gang. He'd seen what they could do to boys who didn't dance to their tune.

"I saw him writin' in a book, and when he weren't lookin', I snuck in there and took me a peek at it. If he hadn't come back when he did, I'd-a got it outta there."

"Why didn't you just take it and run?" *Since you're so brave and bad,* he finished silently.

" 'Cause the book was too big to stuff in my shirt. I didn't want him to know I had it." Shaking his head, he snorted. "You know what's in it?"

"What."

"Poems! Think what would happen to his reputation if folks knew he wrote rhymes!"

"Why should anybody care what he writes in a book?"

"I care," Bobby said through clenched teeth. "He beat my pa once. Bet you didn't know that."

Adam shook his head. "No. I didn't know that." And shrugging, he added. "Why would your pa want to fight him, anyway? Everybody knows he can't be beat." *Dumbness must run in your family,* Adam added mentally.

"My pa coulda whupped him. But he cheated."

"He cheated?" Adam narrowed one eye. "How did he cheat?"

"Well, I don't rightly know; I weren't there. But my pa said he cheated."

And everybody knows your pa doesn't lie. He cheats and steals and kisses the barmaids when he thinks your ma ain't lookin', but of course, he wouldn't think of lying! "How long ago did he fight your pa?"

"Three years, give or take a month."

"And he's still holdin' a grudge?"

Bobby grabbed a fistful of Adam's shirt. "He took my pa's pay, cheatin' that day. We had to sell our best cow to pay the rent."

Adam nodded. "Oh," he choked out.

Bobby released his grip. "Now folks think my pa ain't as strong as him." He jabbed a finger into the air. "Well, I got proof of what he is."

"What is he?"

"My pa says he's a Nancy-boy. He says that's why he cheated. And now we got black and white proof of it. When we show folks that book of poems, they'll know it, too."

Adam had read a few poems in his day, some in school, some from his mother's books. He didn't see anything wrong with writing or reading rhymes.

"So what do you need me for?"

"You're the one who's over there all the time, workin' off that debt. You could get the book and—"

"Me? Why me? You already know where it is."

"You know that big tool box in the back of his warehouse? The one with all the big saws and awls in it?"

Adam nodded.

"Well, it's in the table underneath it. In the right-hand drawer." Bobby gave Adam's back a playful smack. "Now you know where it is, too. You can get it, right now, while he's havin' fun at the festival."

"I—I don't think I wanna."

Bobby's grin became a grimace. "Nobody cares what you wanna do, you mama's boy. I'm tellin' you what you're gonna do."

Adam glared at him. "Why should I?"

" 'Cause if you don't, somethin' awful could happen."

"Like what?"

"Like maybe your ma's shop might catch fire."

"You better not hurt my ma!" he shouted, breathing a little fire of his own.

"I ain't sayin' I will, and I ain't sayin' I won't."

Adam did his best to hide his fear and shock. "Anything happens to her, I'll—"

"You'll what, pip-squeak?"

Flustered, he said in a loud, trembling voice, "I don't know what, but—"

The bigger boy's hand clamped over Adam's mouth, effectively silencing him. "Don't mess with me, mama's boy. I don't say things 'less I mean 'em." He paused, noting the terror that had widened Adam's eyes still further. "That's right. I burned that house the first time."

He seemed so proud to have done such a despicable thing. "You did not," he said against Bobby's hand.

"Think what you will. Don't change the facts."

"But why would you?"

"Old man Norris killed my dog, that's why." He unhanded Adam and helped him up. "Now git on over to the warehouse, while the Irishman is busy moonin' over your ma."

Adam glanced in the direction Bobby had pointed, saw J. J. standing behind his mother. What had O'Keefe said that put that dreamy, happy smile on her face?

Bobby gave him a rough shove. "G'wan, git! And don't come back 'til you've got that book, y'hear?"

He knew Bobby well enough to believe the fire had not been an idle threat. If he said he'd burn the shop, he'd do it.

Adam glanced toward the pines, where O'Keefe now stood alone. He was nearly as big around as the old tree, and the boy knew from watching him work, his muscles were as hard as its trunk. If folks read the book, and started calling him a Nancy-boy, J. J. could handle himself.

Even if he couldn't, being called a name—even one as insulting as that—wasn't as bad as having your home and business burned down.

His boots seemed to be weighted down with lead as he stepped into the clearing and onto the road. Head hanging and shoulders slumped, Adam headed for the warehouse.

Right-hand drawer in the table near the back.

Sorry, J. J., he said to himself. *Sorry.*

five

As eventide shrouded the sunshine, a quietness settled over Currituck.

Main Street was deserted now, save the occasional chirp of a bird and the panting of a stray dog, sniffing out scraps under the now-bare food table. The bandstand that had been throbbing and thumping with knee-slapping music sat silent, a shiny brass tuba, a silver slide trombone, a battered bugle the only evidence that, hours ago, it had been home to toe-tapping music. The booths where kisses had cost a penny, and three cents bought the buyer a chance to dunk a fellow Curritucker, stood side-by-side, empty. The basket responsible for adding three whole dollars toward the purchase of a new organ lay on its side, bright red bow askew, fried chicken and corn bread contents long ago devoured by Pete Stanford, highest bidder in the boxed lunch auction. A crow hip-hopped in the dirt, wrestling with a length of twine that had bound fathers' right ankles to sons' left in the two-legged race. And a yellow-striped cat snoozed contentedly on a tablecloth forgotten by the pastor's wife.

For the moment, the street that had been teeming with activity and echoing with voices, rested, for families had returned to their homes to await the final phase of the Fourth of July festivities: Fireworks!

A stranger passing through town, glancing into the windows of the houses along Main Street might see that in the Adams' house, a toddler and his infant brother napped in the parlor. The Williamses had gathered around the table for a light snack. The Reverend and Mrs. Hall were in the church, setting out the new hymnals. Miss Henderson was in the

94

schoolhouse, taking inventory of the materials she'd need when school started in the fall.

And Adam Flynn lay stomach-down across his bed, a thick, leather-bound journal propped against his pillow, reading. The first entry was dated January 1, 1830. He squinted one eye and pursed his lips. "It's about time he started actin' his age," Mary said when she witnessed "The Kiss." "Man's thirty-five years old. If he doesn't start a family soon, his young'uns will still be in diapers when they attend his funeral!"

If it's 1855, and he's thirty-five now, Adam ciphered, he was ten when he wrote this poem. Flattening the page with the palm of his hand, he propped his chin on a doubled-up fist and read silently:

> *She is twilight and moonlight,*
> *   she is sun on the waters.*
> *She is rain clouds and blue skies,*
> *   she is God's sons and daughters.*
> *She is mountains and valleys,*
> *   she is rivers and loughs.*
> *She is sheep on the hillsides,*
> *   she is cows on the roads.*
> *Rising from the Atlantic,*
> *   she is proud, she is grand.*
> *She is endless beauty,*
> *   she is my Ireland.*

Adam rolled onto his back, taking the book with him. *You made a mistake,* he told himself. *A ten year old couldn't have written a poem that good!* He did the subtraction again, his fingertip drawing the numerals on his pillow this time. The sum was the same: J. J. had been ten when he wrote the rhyme.

Adam shook his head. He'd acknowledged that J. J. was a smart man, what with the way he could handle a measuring stick and figure out how to make ends meet. But he'd obviously been a smart boy, too. June 5, 1841 was the date on this passage, written when the Irishman was twenty-one:

> Last week I was the honored guest of sweet Mary
> McGuire, who wore a long white satin dress to wed
> Tim McIntire. The preacher wished them children, a
> long and happy life, and led us all in prayer for Tim
> and his new wife:
> "They'll need our prayers," the reverend said,
> "to face the road ahead."
> They'll need money for a house and food; I
> prayed for that instead. I didn't hear the sermon. (I
> wonder what I missed.) I didn't hear them say their
> vows, or see them when they kissed. But I saw the
> looks she gave me as she spoke her final vow, 'twas
> a look that's bound to haunt me dreams just as it
> haunts me now: She told me with her clear blue
> eyes that Tim was second choice; that he saw her
> send the message gave me reason to rejoice. For
> I'd come a whisker's breadth from standin' where
> Tim stood. And if I had, 'twould be my face that
> blushed bright red with blood.
> I made a vow right there and then: "Don't ever
> take a wife, for surely you'll regret it all your natural life." If in a weak-kneed moment, I should give
> my heart away, May the Good Lord numb me brain
> and soul, until me dyin' day!

Chuckling under his breath, Adam whispered, "Atta way, J. J.!" He turned to the last entry, written July 3, 1855:

> Dear God,
> You know that I stepped into the ring with powerful men, men who looked as though they had the

*brains and the brawn to put me down. But they
didn't. You know I had no bone to pick, no ax to
grind, no reason to want to see them harmed. And
yet I harmed them. You made me strong. And I
lifted my fists, bare-knuckled, and crouched my
body, bare-chested, and looked into their eyes.
Eyes gleaming with hatred. Or determination. Or
fear. And I swung with all my might, because I
knew no other way. "Do your level best or don't
waste your time." It was one of the best lessons
my father ever taught me. And I'll remember it
always, all the days of my life. You know why I
fought to win: so much was riding on it. To lose
was unthinkable, because to lose, was to admit
defeat, a word I've never understood. You know I
don't know any way, other than to fight with all the
fight You gave me to fight for what I want for what
I need. But until now, the fighting has been easy,
because I haven't wanted or needed anything more
than solitude. Peace. Contentment that comes
from remembering Ireland. You know that until
now, I haven't needed a woman to complete me,
because, until now, I hadn't met one who could.
But that was before Kate. I looked into her eyes
and into her heart and all the cold places in me
warmed.*

Adam closed the book, gently and quietly, and set it aside.
J. J. is in love with Ma, he told himself. *He's in love with your
mother!*

He didn't know quite how to react. For one thing, if Bobby
hadn't threatened him into stealing the journal, he wouldn't
have the information. They'd arrested Victor Wilson last year
for sneaking peeks into first-floor windows all over town. A
"peeping Tom" they'd called him—though he hadn't seen

anything but pies, cooling on window ledges and damp tea towels draped across sills to dry—and made him spend a night in jail. Vic had been so ashamed, he'd left town that very next day, and no one had seen nor heard from the grizzled old fellow since.

Adam didn't have to be a full-grown man to know what he'd done was wrong, far more unacceptable than looking into people's houses. Because folks didn't do things out in the open they didn't want people to see, didn't say things near their windows they didn't want folks to hear.

J. J. had not intended these words to be read. Would there be sketches of trees, and lambs, and horses if he'd wanted others to read his most private thoughts?

Would there be drawings of his mother, smiling, praying, staring off into space? Oh, J. J. loved her. If the poem didn't prove it, the pictures surely did.

He'd watched as Currituck's eligible bachelors—those never-married and those recently widowed—had tried to woo and win her. She'd done it gently, of course, for that was her way, but Kate had turned them down nonetheless. Until he'd learned the truth about his father, Adam had assumed she'd said "no" to remarriage because she was still in love with her husband.

That day when J. J. had followed him home, demanding repayment for the stolen lunches? She hadn't noticed, and neither had Mary, but Adam had been sitting on the stairs that very evening, listening as his mother poured her heart out. There was a long, oval mirror in one corner of the shop, where ladies and gentlemen could see how fine they looked in the garments she sewed for them. He could see her face in that mirror, as the story of her past unfolded: She'd hadn't rejected the proposals because was still in love with Sean, she'd turned the men down because she'd never loved him.

If he'd heard it once, he'd heard it a million-zillion times,

Adam believed: "My, but your ma has the prettiest eyes!" He agreed, not because they were big and brown, but because they looked at him with such love, warm like the fields after a late spring planting. Her eyes had narrowed, darkened with fear when she'd spoken of Sean. Not so when she talked about J. J. Especially not so when she talked to him!

True enough, Adam was a long way off from becoming a full-grown man. But he knew enough to recognize love when he saw it. His mother had not written poetry about O'Keefe, nor had she drawn pictures of the Irishman (at least, not to his knowledge), but like the grown-ups were so fond of saying, "It's plain as the nose on your face!"

Would they get married? And if they did, would they live here, in the apartment above his ma's dress shop, or in the rooms over J. J.'s warehouse? Here, he hoped, because although J. J.'s living quarters were clean and tidy, they were hardly homey.

It might be nice, having a pa for the first time in his life, a man he could go to for advice, a fellow who would understand when the girls at school passed notes across the classroom that said "I like you. Do you like me?"

His heartbeat quickened as he added, someone who would know how to handle a boy like Bobby. He hadn't wanted to take the book. But he hadn't wanted Bobby to burn down the dress shop even more.

He shouldn't have taken the journal. He knew that even before he'd tiptoed into the warehouse, even before he'd slunk toward the worktable where J. J. had hidden it in a drawer. But now that he'd done it, it was too late to make it right.

Wasn't it?

"You know right from wrong, son," his mother had often said. "And on the occasions when you aren't sure what's right and what's wrong, ask yourself what I would advise you to do, and do that."

Adam sat up with a start, and headed for the stairs, quoting another cliché favored by old folks: "It's never too late."

He would put the journal back where he'd found it, and pretend he'd never trespassed into J. J.'s most secret thoughts and keep a mighty close eye on Bobby from here on out.

ঞ

"What're ye doin' back there, Adam?"

With quaking hands and hammering heart, he shoved the book back into its proper place and quickly closed the drawer. "Snooping around," he said, opening the tool box on the workbench. "I like looking at your tools."

J. J. grinned. "Well, shut the lid when ye're done gawkin', then, to keep the sawdust off 'em, will ye?"

"Sure." He hesitated. "Say, J. J., did you ever have a run-in with a bully?"

"Adam," he said, smiling, "when I was a lad, I was the bully."

The boy's blue eyes widened. "Really?"

"Nah. I'm just funnin' with ye." He could see that the boy was serious and more than just a little afraid. "Somebody givin' ye a hard time, are they?"

He frowned, pocketed his hands. "Sorta. Well, not exactly."

"But ye were just wonderin' how ye would handle a bully in case ye ever find yerself face to face with one down the road someday."

"Yeah! That's it." The light in his eyes faded. "So what would you do if you ran into a bully?"

J. J. perched on the corner of his battered old desk. "Well, now, let me see," he said, combing his fingers through is beard. "First off, I guess I'd try and figure out if the bully is really worth bein' afraid of." He met Adam's eyes. "Is yer bully bigger than ye?"

"Uh-huh. But that's not why I'm scared of him."

J. J. pretended he hadn't heard the boy's outright admission. "Then he must be holdin' somethin' over yer head."

Adam nodded.

"Ye have to ask yerself, then, is he the type who might carry it out, or is he all bark and no bite."

"All bark and no bite? What does that mean?"

Chuckling, J. J. explained. "It means he's heavy on the threats, and light on the follow-through."

"Well, I don't know what sort of trouble he's gotten into lately, but he says he's done some terrible things in the past."

"What sort of things?"

"Well, for one thing, he says it was him that burned down the house Ma and me live in now. Says he did it 'cause the man who used to live there killed his dog."

J. J. had heard about that fire. It had been set in the middle of the night, while the family slept. Old man Norris's daughter had just buried her husband and had moved back in with her father until she could find a job to support her three youngsters. No one had made it out of that house alive.

"I wasn't here at the time, of course, but old man Norris did have a bit of a temper, way I hear it. But even if he did kill the boy's dog, 'twasn't reason enough to—" J. J. stopped himself. He didn't know how much Adam had heard about the tragedy. *No sense givin' the lad nightmares,* he told himself.

"So you think so? You think he might do it again?"

"I don't know, Adam. Is that what he told you? Did he say he'd set another fire?"

"He said if I didn't. . .he'd—" He sighed, nodded again.

"Then, first order of business is to find out if he's really guilty of settin' the first fire."

"Why would he say something like that if he didn't do it?"

"Some folks need so much attention, Adam, that even bein' thought of as a firebug is better than not bein' thought of at all."

Adam shook his head, ran a hand through his hair. "How will we find out if he set the Norris's house on fire or not?"

"Well, we could start at the sheriff's office. Ernie has been in town nearly his whole life. If anybody'd know, he would."

The boy stared at some unknown point beyond J. J.'s left shoulder. "But if he did it, why isn't he in jail? People died in that fire!"

"Ye've got a good point there. Surely there'd have been talk about a thing like that. And that kind of talk doesn't fade away. Bad news has a life of its own, don't ye know."

"Then we may never find out for sure if he was just makin' it up, or if he really did it."

"Ye might could trick him."

"Trick him?"

"Ask questions. Where'd he start the fire? What did he use for fuel? What time was it when he lit the match—if he even used a match."

Adam was taking it all in, as evidenced by his narrowed eyes, his thinned lips, his furrowed brow.

"Did he tell ye what he'd burn?"

"Ma's dress shop," he said, his voice trembling.

And J. J.'s heart thudded against his ribs. "Why would he want to do a thing like that? Yer ma never did a wrong thing in all her life."

"He wants—he said he wants me to–to get somethin' for him."

"Somethin' that ain't yers, I'm guessin'."

Guilt darkened the blue of his eyes, but J. J. couldn't for the life of him understand what Adam would have to feel guilty about.

"Uh-huh."

He raised one brow. "The way he wanted ye to get, oh, say, a certain lunch bucket?"

Adam's eyes widened with fear. "Don't ask me to tell you who he is, J. J.," he said after a moment, " 'cause I wouldn't want to lie to you, but I wouldn't want the rest of the boys thinkin' I'm a snitch, either. Besides, he'd just deny it if you asked him what his part was in it."

It didn't matter if Adam named the boy or not. What he didn't say told J. J. all he needed to know, and he knew exactly whom Adam was afraid of and why.

He'd seen the brat around town, strutting up and down the street like a Banty rooster. He'd put as much effort into developing his reputation as a bad boy as most folks put into their jobs. If Bobby had made a threat, it was entirely possible he would carry it out. He had to be stopped, somehow.

And he said exactly that.

"It was my ma he threatened, it oughta be me who stops him."

"I admire yer courage, but ye're not dealin' with an ordinary boy, here. If he's guilty of killin' those people, he's the Devil personified. He's evil through and through. No tellin' what he might do to ye."

"I'll be careful." He thought a moment. "I'll make sure I'm never alone with him. That way, he can't hurt me."

"I'll be keepin' a close eye on ye, nonetheless," J. J. promised. "Ye have a day, no more. After that, I'll take matters into me own hands."

"But J. J.," Adam protested, "he already thinks I'm a mama's boy."

"What a malicious hard-hearted—" He stopped himself. "Doesn't matter what he thinks of ye, Adam. All that matters is what you think when ye look in the mirror. I'm all in favor of yer standin' up to him, 'cause if ye don't, ye'll be runnin' from him all yer life."

When the boy's cheeks paled with fear, he put a hand on his shoulder, gave it an affectionate squeeze. "There's a chance yer bully will be so surprised that anybody would face him down, he'll leave ye be, just out of respect for yer bravery."

A glimmer of hope lit Adam's eyes.

"But it's only fair to warn ye: There's just as good a chance he'll whomp ye, whomp ye hard, and do it in front of his chums to teach the lot of ye not to cross him." He hesitated, to give the idea time to register. "Ye're the only one who can decide which way to go."

Adam sighed.

"Let me tell ye a little story, lad."

J. J. pointed at the chair beside the desk, and when Adam sat in it, he said, "When I first came to town, I kept runnin' into a fellow who didn't like me much."

"But why? Everybody I know likes you."

He smiled. "Thank ye, lad, for the kind words. But 'twasn't always that way. I had to earn the respect of the good people of Currituck."

"Is he still here? Does he live here now?"

"That he does. And he'd heard what I used to do for a living, that I had been a professional boxer. For a reason I still haven't figured out, 'twas a fact that bothered him. He never let me pass by without makin' some sort of rude noise or crude comment about me past. The gist of it was he didn't believe a big dumb Mick like me had the brains to be The Annihilator."

"What's a 'Mick'? Adam wanted to know.

J. J. smiled fondly. "Yer innocence sometimes astounds me, lad."

The boy's nose crinkled with confusion. "Huh?"

Chuckling, J. J. said, " 'Mick' is what some folks call the Irish when they want to insult 'em."

"Why?"

" 'Cause so many of our names begin with a 'Mc' this or a 'Mc' that; in Irish, it means 'son of,' y' know."

"Yours doesn't."

"True enough. Just goes to show ye how little sense words like that can make."

J. J. continued his story.

"So anyway, I paid this fella no mind at first, and for a couple of months, I managed to ignore him. But he must have gotten bored, hittin' me with nothin' but words, and he took to hittin' me with his hands. 'I'll not fight ye, man,' I told him. He'd riled me but good, and I could clearly see that he was out to become a local legend for takin' down The Annihilator. But I'd fought for a livin'; what if I hurt him, hurt him bad?

"Well, anyway, before long, not even the physical stuff was satisfyin' to him, and one day he took a mind to sock me in the jaw. Just like that, without a word of warnin'. Caught me off guard, he did, knocked me on me backside. I could see right then, while I was lyin' flat on me back lookin' up at the blue sky, that it'd go on and on this way if I didn't put a stop to it."

"Did you beat him senseless?"

"Oh, I could've hit him, maybe even put him six feet under. But I gave him the evil eye. Shamed him. Acted like his fist didn't hurt a bit. And to tell ye the truth, Adam, with the vicious anger boilin' in me, it didn't.

"So I got to me feet and dusted off the seat of me pants, and told him if it was a fight he wanted, it was a fight he'd get. But it'd be a fair fight, a clean fight. We'd put on the gloves and have it out in the ring, with an official judge, and witnesses, the works. He didn't like the idea, of course, 'cause he preferred gettin' in his licks on the sly. But the men in town taunted him 'til he agreed to it. 'If ye win,' I told him, 'I'll leave town if that's what ye want; but if I win, ye'll promise to stay clear of me.'

"Now, mind ye, I knew full well that he had a reputation for bein' a cheat and a liar. I didn't figure him for the type who'd go by the book. And he was a big man, too, way bigger'n me. He could've done me poor old body a lot of damage, permanent damage, if he sneaked in one of his cheatin' punches. But if I didn't face him, he would've done permanent harm to me good name. Me da and his da before him were dead and buried, and I wasn't about to let the likes of some ruffian tarnish the family name. So we set a date and took off our shirts."

Unable to keep quiet a moment longer, Adam blurted out, "It was Bobby's father, wasn't it?"

"It was."

"And you beat the stuffin's out of him, didn't you?"

J. J. aimed a calmly stern glance at the boy. "I won the fight, that I did, but I won somethin' more important that day, Adam. I won me freedom from his bullyin'. 'Twas a prize worth far more than any money I'd earned in the ring."

"But J. J., if he was a liar and a cheat, how did you know he'd keep his word? How did you know he wouldn't just get out of the ring and go right back to treating you the way he had been before the fight?"

"I didn't know. Least, I didn't know for sure. I could only hope and pray that shame would keep him walkin' straight and true. Most of the men in town had heard him strike the bargain, y' see. So if he had gone back on his word, he would have looked like a fool to the lot of 'em, and his bullyin' days would be over for sure."

"You mean he never bothered anybody again?"

J. J. chuckled. "I don't think I put an end to his bullyin', but I kept it out of my backyard. 'Cause, y' see, a bully will always find a willing victim to pick on. 'Tis part of his nature. But to answer yer question, well, that's a matter of degree. Just seein' the man 'bothers' me, to this very day. But he hasn't said a cross word, nor has he laid a rough hand on me since the fight. He stuck by his part of the deal, thank God, and me life's better for it."

He'd given the boy a lot to think about, as evidenced by the deep furrows lining his otherwise smooth brow. " 'A wrathful man stirreth up strife; but he that is slow to anger appeaseth strife.' "

"I didn't know you read the Bible, J. J."

"I don't." Kate was a true believer, and she was trying to

raise Adam to be a follower as well. She would not approve of him sharing his opinions about the Good Book with her son. "I don't read the Word as often as I should, I admit, but I know this: God doesn't intend for us to stand idly by and let others run roughshod over us."

"Why?"

"Haven't ye ever heard that your body is His temple."

"Yes."

"Well?"

"I get it, J. J. Thanks."

Adam headed for the door, hesitated just inside it. "Will I see you at the fireworks later?"

"Wouldn't miss it for all the world."

He watched Adam walk away standing a little taller than when he came into the warehouse.

❧

He'd never seen anything quite so beautiful.

Oh, he'd watched a fireworks show before. Three times before, to be exact. *And they say the Irish know how to kick up their heels and celebrate!* he thought each year as the sky shimmered with rainbow hues. But the giant, glimmering flowers that bloomed, then rained their sparkling petals upon the earth were nothing in comparison to the shine in Kate Flynn's eyes.

"Where did they get the canisters this year?" Mary asked, taking his attention from Kate's face.

"Don't rightly know, Mother." When the last ember of the lustrous light faded, Thaddius glanced away from the sky show to look at his wife. "You're glowin' like a schoolgirl," he said, and kissed her full on the mouth.

"Goodness, Thaddius," Mary giggled.

"If it weren't so dark," he teased affectionately, "folks would see me blushin' all the way across the street!"

Leaning forward on the blanket they'd shared with the elderly couple, J. J. whispered, "Will the two of ye rein it in a bit?" he teased. "There are children all around, don't ye know?"

Thaddius grinned. "I believe these fireworks came straight from China," he said, branding J. J. with a teasingly withering glare.

"But honey, aren't all fireworks made in China?"

He shrugged. "Most of 'em are, that's true. But I heard-tell that some feller by the name of Homer Jones ordered himself a whole passel of 'em last July, then jacked up the price, tellin' town council he was savin' 'em the bother of orderin' and shippin' and what-not."

Mary gasped, watched the next explosion that lit the night sky. "But are they safe after all this time?"

"Fireworks ain't never foolproof," he said knowledgeably. "You might say each one is a bomb."

As the old folks discussed the matter further, Kate lay on her side, her head propped on her palm. "Isn't it romantic?" she asked on a sigh.

J. J. met her eyes. "The fireworks, y'mean?"

"Well, in a manner of speaking." Kate hid a tiny giggle behind her free hand. "Mary and Thaddius; I think it's wonderful, the way they behave after all their time together."

So, he thought, *she's envious of 'em, too.*

"I wonder," she said dreamily, looking into the sky. Her face reflected the overhead light.

"What do ye wonder?"

Her eyes were wide with wonder and tenderness when she looked into his. "What's their secret?"

"Secret?"

She nodded. "How have they kept that–that spark alive all these years?"

He wanted to wrap his arms around her, crush her to him, press a hungry kiss to her lips.

" 'Tis no secret. Leastways, not in my opinion."

Kate sat up, folded her legs Indian style, and clasped her hands in her lap. "Go on," she coaxed, "what is your opinion?"

He leaned back, fingers splayed on the blanket, stiffened arms acting as braces to hold him up. "There's nothin' mysterious about it," he said matter-of-factly. "They were right for one another. It's as simple as that."

She scooted closer. "But it can't be as simple as that. All around the world, people get married every day, and I imagine every couple believes they're right for each other."

J. J. shook his head. "I disagree. It's my belief that folks know when they've found the mate God has chosen for 'em and they know when they haven't."

"How do they know?"

Using his thumb as a pointer, he gestured toward the sky. "He tells 'em if they take the time to ask."

Kate smiled. "You surprise me."

One brow rose slightly as he grinned. "And why is that?"

"I never imagined you were the type. . ."

He filled her hesitation with a question. "What type?"

"The religious type."

His grin ebbed to a smile. "Just 'cause a man doesn't spend every Sunday at services doesn't mean he's a heathen, Kate."

"Doesn't mean he isn't, either," she countered, raising a brow of her own.

They watched the next three fireworks in companionable silence. As the men who were lighting fuses from a barge in the sound prepared the next explosion, Kate said, "Have you ever asked, J. J.?"

Eyes focused on the sky, he said, "Have I ever asked what?"

"If a particular lady was right for you?"

He looked into her face. "I should-a, once, and didn't."

"Disastrous?"

"That's puttin' it mildly."

She sent him a sad smile. "I should-a once, too, and didn't."

"Yer husband, ye mean?"

Kate nodded. "My keeper is more like it. I thought I was doing the right thing, a good thing." She shrugged. "Turns out it was bad for everybody, Sean included."

"Bad for Sean?" J. J. couldn't believe his ears. "He got the prettiest wife in Americay, and the most lovin', too."

She shook her head and started to protest.

"Hush, now," he told her, " 'cause I'll not listen while ye dismiss the truth. Ye did a good and lovin' thing, marryin' that no-good Irishman to save yer family. 'Twasn't yer fault things turned out the way they did."

Kate tilted her head slightly. "I appreciate your coming to my defense, J. J., but the fact is, I never asked God's opinion in the matter. Made the decision, just like that." She snapped her fingers. "I wonder how different things would have been if—"

"If," he said. "Takes but two letters to spell the biggest word in the English language."

She sighed. "I suppose you're right."

"I know I'm right. I'm always right. Just ask."

A second ticked by before they broke out in peals of delighted laughter.

"Say, what's goin' on back there?" Thaddius wanted to know.

"You're making more racket than the fireworks," Mary said.

"You know, Mary," Kate said, catching her breath, "you're absolutely right."

"I know I'm right."

Eyes gleaming with mischief, Kate and J. J. looked at one another and bit their lips.

"I'm always right."

They couldn't forestall it, not even with hands pressed over their mouths.

"Just ask—"

The laughter drowned out Mary's last word.

"Thaddius."

And the tears in their eyes kept them from seeing the puzzled expression on Mary's face. The old woman looked at her husband, drew a circle in the air beside her temple, and rolled her eyes.

"Young folks these days," Thaddius said.

And when Kate and J. J. burst into a whole new round of laughter, he looked even more confused than his wife.

ta

"Hey!" shouted Burt Garfield. "You boys get away from there!" The big, burly fellow stomped toward Bobby and his gang, as if intent upon picking them up by the scruffs of their necks and tossing them boots-over-brains into the water. "Don't you realize we're working with explosives here? Gunpowder?" he said, accenting the word for emphasis.

"We weren't gonna touch nothin', mister," Bobby said. "We just wanted to see how you get them rockets to go so high in the sky."

"Wait 'til you're older, and you can volunteer to light the fuses."

"But, mister—"

"But nothing! These are pyrotechnics, boys. One wrong move, and we can be blown to smithereens. Now get a-move on," he threatened, shaking a huge fist at them, "before I show you exactly how those rockets go so high in the sky."

Bobby narrowed his eyes and studied his options. He could go around the big lummox—and risk being dragged home by his ear—or he could bide his time. Smiling, he shrugged.

"C'mon," he said to his gang, "Mr. Garfield is right. We could get hurt if we hang around here."

Burt smiled. "Now there's a sensible fella." He winked. "You can see the fireworks better from a distance, anyway." He leaned forward, pressed the side of his hand to his mouth and whispered, "All you see from this vantage point is the fiery tail of the rocket; you're so busy squinting and covering up your ears to keep from having to listen to that awful squeal, you miss the good part."

Bobby frowned. Grown-ups. Each one's dumber than the

next. "Why do you do it, then?"

"Somebody's got to do it. I've been enjoying the show every July Fourth for twenty-odd years. Just seems fitting and proper to give back a bit of that enjoyment." And satisfied that he'd convinced the boys to move back to a place of safety, he added, "Now get on down the hill. We're about to set the fuses for the finale."

The finale, Bobby grumbled inwardly. Big deal. But he grinned and led his gang away from the row of hollow metal pipes that would act like mini-cannons for the fireworks' canisters. When they were out of Burt's line of vision, he signaled the boys to duck into a stand of trees.

"Hunker down here a minute while I figure out what to do," he whispered.

"I dunno, Bobby," Stevie said, "maybe we oughta do what old Burt says. I don't wanna get blown to Kingdom Come."

Bobby sneered. "What's the matter, baby?" he began, grabbing Stevie's shirt collar.

Without taking his eyes off the boy, he said to the rest of the gang, "I think the widdo baby forgot to bwing his widdo bottle." And nose-to-nose with smaller boy, he tightened his hold. "Is that it? Huh? Did you forget to bring your bottle?"

"Stop it," Stevie whimpered. "I'm not a baby."

"Then what's your problem? Are you scared? Are you yeller, like that Nancy-boy, Adam Flynn?"

"Who you callin' a Nancy-boy?"

All eyes turned from Bobby and Stevie to focus on the speaker.

"Well if it isn't Adam Flynn," Bobby said, "son of the village harlot."

Harlot? Adam didn't even know what the word meant, but from Bobby's tone and expression, he knew it meant something vile and ugly. "You take that back."

"Make me," the bigger boy challenged.

"My mother's not a har–a–what you said."

Stevie stood as close to Adam as he could.

And Bobby snickered. "Then what's she doin' kissin' a man in the middle of Main Street for everybody to see? My ma says she's a wanton hussy. My pa says she's a—"

Adam stepped up to his opponent and filled his hands with the boy's shirt. "I don't care what your ma and pa say. She's my mother. Now you take it back before—"

Bobby's eyes widened with surprise at the younger boy's words and actions. He looked down at Adam's hands. "If you know what's good for you, you'll turn me loose."

"Take it back, and I'll let go," he said through clenched teeth.

Bobby cocked a fist, but Adam was faster, wrapping his fingers around the boy's wrist.

Grinning nervously, he said to his gang, "The pip-squeak is pretty quick, ain't he?"

The boys did not respond.

"Let go, you miserable little booger eater, or—"

Adam didn't move, save the narrowing of his eyes. "Or what?"

"Or I'll turn your face into pulp."

"Is that what happened to your face? Somebody beat it into pulp?"

"Listen to him," Bobby snapped. "The boy whose ma is a harlot and whose pa got shot cheatin' at cards."

"Yeah, and I hear that he sometimes got so riled up, it took three, four men to pull him off a man twice his size."

"So?"

"So folks say I'm an awful lot like him."

Bobby thought that one over for a moment. "You're awfully brave for a little squirt who's about to get the beating of his life."

Adam shrugged one shoulder. "Not brave. Determined."

Bobby's brow furrowed. "Huh?"

"I only fight when I know I can win."

"Win! You? Don't make me laugh." He turned to his buddies. "He's a real gut-buster, ain't he?"

Again, the boys said nothing.

Bobby faced Adam. "Did you get the book?" he asked changing he subject.

"Uh-huh."

"You did not."

"Yes, I did."

"Then where is it?"

"I put it back."

"You did what?"

"I put it back."

"Liar. You never got it in the first place, 'cause you're yeller."

"Blue book, 'bout this big," Adam said, hands several inches apart.

Bobby sneered. "All right, so you went in there and saw it. That don't mean you had it."

"With a red stripe down the left side."

"You really had it?"

"Uh-huh."

"Then why'd you put it back? I told you to bring it to me. I told you we were gonna—"

"You're not the boss of me. I don't have to do what you say."

A myriad of emotions flickered over Bobby's face frustration, fury, fear. He wriggled free of Adam's grasp, backed up, and stood amid his pals. "We're missin' the fireworks. Let's get out of here."

The boys, some with hands pocketed, some with arms crossed over their chests, sauntered past Adam and Stevie. Frankie hesitated, his gaze wavering between amazement and admiration, as if unable to decide whether to stay, or head out with Bobby and the others. Head down and shoulders slumped, he shuffled along with the rest of them.

Bobby didn't repeat his threat to set fire to the dress shop, Adam noted. He hoped J. J. was right, that the boy was all bark and no bite. Because his mother would pay a terrible price if the Irishman was wrong.

❧

"Somethin's wrong," J. J. said, peering into darkness. "I can feel it in me bones."

Kate sat up. "I didn't see anything."

" 'Tisn't what I saw that's botherin' me, 'tis what I heard. That last one. 'Twas different from the rest."

She was on her knees now, elbows cupped in her palms, looking for the source of his distress. "The last what was different?"

"What's goin' on back there?" Thaddius grumped, turning.

"You two make as much noise as a couple of teenagers," Mary agreed.

At the same moment in time, the elderly couple's smiles disappeared as they read J. J.'s face. "What is it, son?"

Thaddius never got his answer.

J. J. stood, crouched and ready for what, no one knew.

"Hey, down in front!"

"It's like tryin' to see around the side of a movin' barn," someone else grumbled.

But J. J. never heard the complaints. "Somethin's wrong," he said again. "It sounded—"

Suddenly, a bright flash, a loud explosion, an agonized bellow, quickly followed by another blast, and another.

"The fireworks canisters." J. J. was off and running before any of them could question the statement.

He thundered across the grass, the sand, big booted feet splashing over the water's edge as he headed for the place where Burt and his fellow volunteers were setting off the fireworks.

"Stay back, O'Keefe!" a man shouted as he passed.

"There's nothin' you can do for him," someone else hollered. "You go in there, you'll end up in the same fix!" But he paid them no mind.

In the fleeting seconds it took to cover the last bit of ground, his mind whirled back, back in time, remembering.

Years ago, in Ireland, one of his pals had somehow gotten hold of a small, ancient cannon. Connor's rage had been infectious, and spread through the countryside like the fever. Armed with nothing more than crude weapons—hand-forged pikes, knives, clubs, rocks—they practiced a week, running the defensive maneuvers the Pikesmen would employ against the English. They had but a dozen cannonballs; no one knew how old they were, but they couldn't afford not to test at least one. He'd been young and healthy and strong, and so he'd been assigned to move the thing from place to place. He'd ducked, forearms over head and facing the dirt like everyone else when the "Ready, fire!" call was sounded. Ducked, and waited.

He could still smell the stench of sulfur after the match was lit, could still hear the fizzling, sizzling sound of the burning wick. But something was wrong. He turned, expecting to see that Connor had forgotten to shorten the wick and squinted instead in instinctual response to the eye-blinding burst of light, clapped his hands to his ears to muffle the deafening, discharge.

When the smoke cleared, Connor lay flat on his back, arms akimbo. It was a grisly, bloody site, one that made every man there grimace and turn away. Some ended up in the bushes, retching. Some ended up with their head between their knees, fighting the faint.

He knelt beside his life-long friend. "I'm a goner, John Joseph."

And even young J. J. could see it was true; he couldn't find a place on Connor that wasn't bleeding profusely.

With a strength that belied his condition, Connor clamped

a blood-slicked hand around J. J.'s forearm. "Don't let 'em tell me ma how I ended up; she'll see it in 'er dreams 'til she draws 'er last, sure."

Meeting his buddy's eyes, he choked back a sob, for even his eyes were bloody!

"Promise me, John Joseph. I can't go to God wi' that on me mind." Connor had groaned, gasped, grit his teeth. "and I want to go soon, 'cause there ain't a place on me that don't hurt."

The instant J. J. made the promise, Connor's fingers unclenched, his hand relaxed, and J. J. knew the precise moment in time when his spirit left him, for he'd watched the life-light fade from his eyes.

And now, in the utter quiet that followed the series of explosions, he knelt beside Burt. "What happened, man?"

Burt coughed. "Stuck. Tried to force it. Shouldn't of put my arm in."

What was left of his arm flopped grotesquely on the ground beside him, spurting blood, spattering the men who'd drawn near.

"Are ye daft, man?" J. J. gently asked, tearing out of his shirt. "What were ye thinkin', pokin' yer hand down that shaft?"

Burt managed a feeble grin. "The young'uns. Couldn't disappoint the—"

"Enough," J. J. whispered, smiling slightly as he tied the shirt firmly on Burt's stump to slow the bleeding. "Save yer strength," he added, slipping a stick into the knot and twisting the tourniquet tight, "to explain to Cindy how ye ruined yer best shirt."

Burt smiled a bit, nodded, and closed his eyes.

J. J. slipped his arms under Burt. "He's out cold," J. J. told the small crowd that had gathered, "a small blessin'." With a great groan of effort, he stood, big feet steadily moving across the same ground he'd covered moments ago. "One of ye run ahead and fetch the doctor," he said through clenched teeth, "and one of ye get a bottle of whiskey." He glanced at Burt's face, grimacing in pain even in his unconscious state. " 'Cause he's gonna need all the numbing he can get."

six

"Strange you should ask me that."

J. J. shifted on his chair. "Strange?"

"Well, it's been two, three years since I've heard it mentioned. Then, not two hours ago, a boy comes in here, asking the same questions you're asking now." Sheriff Walker looked up from his whittling to meet J. J.'s eyes. "You can see why I find that strange, can't you?"

J. J. eyed the man warily. What was "strange," in his opinion, was that Ernest Walker wore a tie every day of his life. What was "strange" was that he didn't wear a cap or a Derby or one of those wide-brimmed things the fellows out west were sporting these days, but a tall black hat that put J. J. in mind of a stovepipe. Walker took it off and hung it on one knee, waiting in silence for J. J.'s response.

"I'll be straight with ye, Ernie. One of those ruffians who run roughshod over the town is makin' threats—serious ones—to Adam Flynn."

"Ah, yes," he said, nodding, "Bobby takes the heat for a lot of the bad things that happen in this town."

J. J. frowned. "Well-deserved heat, for the most part, I'd guess. But that's neither here nor there, because Adam never mentioned a name to me, for fear of bein' branded a—" He paused, searching his memory for the word Adam had used.

"A snitch?"

J. J. jabbed a finger into the air. "That's it! He didn't give me a name, for fear of bein' branded a snitch. Well, this boy—whoever he is—asked Adam to do him a, ah, a favor of sorts. And when Adam refused, the little hoodlum said he'd burn down Kate's dress shop."

Walters had been lounging in the high-backed chair, looking as though he'd only been half listening to J. J. He sat up straight and planted both boots on the floor. "He said what?"

"Ye heard me, Ernie. Adam thought maybe the boy was tellin' a tall tale, see, and said so. And this young hooligan cited the Norris fire as proof he had it in him to do such a thing."

The sheriff pursed his lips. "We never did find out who was responsible for that."

"Could it have been an accident?"

"Not a chance. The place reeked of whale oil." He leaned both elbows on his knees, turned his tall silk hat upside down, right-side up, upside down in the space between them. "It was the smell that woke Mary Crofton. If it hadn't been for her caterwauling, there's no telling how much damage could have been done that night. She had the whole town wide awake within fifteen minutes, I'd say. And the men had the fire out a half hour later."

J. J. frowned. "But I heard that Norris and his daughter and grandchildren were burnt up in the blaze."

"That's what most folks think."

"If the fire didn't kill 'em, what did?"

"Oh, the fire killed 'em, all right."

He gave J. J. a quick once-over. "You ever been to Kate's place?"

"Twice," he admitted. "Once in the dress shop, once in the apartment above it."

"Did you get upstairs by way of the back steps?"

J. J. nodded. "Why?"

Walters shrugged. " 'Cause if you'd gone up by way of the inside stairs, you'd have seen that there's a door at the top of the staircase. A door with a big slide-bolt on the outside of it. Whoever set the fire threw the lock first."

Grimacing, J. J. said, "So the lot of 'em were trapped up there."

"Trevor Norris wasn't the kind of man who'd run for mayor." He snickered, twirling one tip of his silvery handlebar mustache between thumb and forefinger. "At least, he wouldn't run and win. He wasn't exactly the sociable type, but he paid his bills and didn't make any trouble. Folks didn't pay much attention to him, one way or the other, and they hadn't had time to decide whether or not they cared for his daughter or her young'uns."

He took another deep breath, sat up straighter. "What did Bobby give as his reason for setting that fire," he asked J. J.

"He said Norris killed his dog."

A look of alarm widened the sheriff's eyes, and put him on his feet. He began pacing the small space between his desk and the wall. "Killed his dog?"

J. J. nodded.

"Strange. I do remember an incident," he began, talking more to himself than to J. J., "when the boy couldn't have been more than eight or nine. Had this mangy, flea-bitten old cur on his heels. Norris was sitting on his porch step, scraping mud off his boot heels with a stick, when this ornery critter comes up and does his business on Trevor's stockinged foot. Well, he jumped up, one boot on, shaking the other, called the animal everything but a dog. It would have taken a bite of him, I believe, if he hadn't given it a good swift kick in the head."

Walker slumped in his battered old chair, tossed his hat onto the desktop. "Dog died two days later; fire happened at the end of that same week." He ran a hand through thinning, graying brown hair. "I never put two and two together," he said, staring at the wall across from him.

"I never had any proof—so I couldn't make an arrest, of course—but I always thought it was that Indian woman who did it. She's crazy as a bedbug."

"Running Deer?"

"Yeah, that's the one all right. Her own people threw her

out of their village, you know, because she's—"

"Crazy as a bedbug," J. J. finished glumly. "I've heard."

"All these years, I was convinced it was her. Every time I see her in town, which isn't often, I'm all over her like white on rice. 'We don't need your kind around here,' I say, and chase her out of town." He shook his head.

"Did anything like it ever happen again?"

"The fire you mean?"

J. J. nodded.

"Nah. Small things, but nothing like that."

"Small things?"

"Eggs on the clapboards, soap on the window glass. Mischief, mostly, except—" His blue eyes darkened as the brows above them knitted in a serious frown. "Stolen purses, and break-ins at the hotel. And," he frowned, "and then there was Miss Henderson's cat."

"Killed?"

Walters nodded. "Somebody set it on fire."

The picture of it flitted through his mind, making J. J. wince. He'd never been overly fond of cats, merely tolerating their presence because they served a useful purpose as ratters. He'd known folks who despised felines. But to kill one, especially that way. *What kind of depraved, demented mind could conjure a torture like that?* he wondered.

For a moment, neither man spoke, and the only sound in the room was the steady tick-tick-ticking of the clock on the wall. "What kind of grades did Miss Henderson give Bobby in school?" J. J. asked.

In place of an answer, the sheriff said, "You're making me look bad, O'Keefe." One side of his mouth lifted in a somber-eyed grin. "You ever get bored, building ships, maybe you ought to think about signing on with Scotland Yard."

"I've had me fill of all things British, Ernie," he admitted, standing, "but thanks for the compliment, just the same."

Walker hadn't heard J. J.'s last remark. "I never put two

and two together," he said to himself. "Who would have thought a boy that young could hate like that?"

❧

He ignored the girls' childish taunts as he headed for the dress shop. The way J. J. figured it, he had it coming, kissing Kate out in the open the way he had yesterday.

"Kate and J. J. sittin' in a tree," they chanted, "k-i-s-s-i-n-g. First comes love. . ." He knew the rhyme as well as anyone, and as he rounded the corner, said the next one to himself. "Then comes marriage, then comes Katie with a baby carriage."

The picture that flashed in his head and made his heart ache with longing.

Stop dreamin' about what you'd like, he told himself. *If ye care anything about Kate at all, ye'll think of her safety and nothin' else right now.*

Hopefully, his plan would do just that.

He had two work shirts, both blue, plus a white one he reserved for special occasions. J. J. needed another like he needed more whiskers in his beard. But since he couldn't think of another excuse to be alone with her—one that wouldn't start lips to flapping, anyway—he decided to have her measure him up for a new one.

She was bent over the work table when he walked into the shop, a fat pencil behind one ear, three or four straight pins between her teeth. The corners of her mouth crinkled in a warm smile when she turned and saw him standing in the doorway. "Mmmm!" she said, and gestured to the chair beside the workbench. "Mmmm-mmmm."

"Hello yerself," J. J. responded, hovering near the door. "Maybe I shouldn't come in; ye look mighty busy."

She stuck the pins into an cushion made to look like an apple. "Don't be silly. I'm never to busy to visit with a friend."

Ah, Kate, he thought, *what I'd give to be more than just yer friend.* "Got me an official invitation to attend Susie Howard's weddin', so I took a look at me only fancy shirt. It's seen better days, I'm afraid."

"You're here to have me sew you a new one?"

He smiled. "Why d'ye look so surprised? It's what ye do for a livin', isn't it?"

"Well, well, yes," she stammered. "It's just I never expected to be—to be measuring you up for—"

He closed the gap between them in three long strides. "If the prospect of bein' that near me causes ye that much apprehension, I suppose I can ride over to Sligo, see if there's a seamstress there who needs the work."

Her cheeks reddened and her eyes widened. "I'm not afraid of you. It's–it's nothing of the kind."

But J. J. knew better. She was afraid, all right, afraid of what people would say if the two of them were seen alone together, again. And who could blame her, after the way they'd behaved on the Fourth!

"Easy, now," he assured, a hand on her shoulder. "I've as much right to be here as any other customer." He pointed. "The door's wide open and so are the curtains."

Kate fidgeted with the lacy trim on her apron pocket, then tucked a loose tendril of hair behind her ear. "I suppose you're right." She took a calming breath. "Tell me, how's Burt?"

"Last I heard, he's healin' up just fine. Ain't none too happy 'bout bein' shy an arm, but he'll come around, I expect."

Pity lifted her brows. "What do you suppose he'll do for a living, now that he only has one arm? He certainly can't be a blacksmith any more."

"Why can't he?"

"Well, it'd be too dangerous, working around the fire and all. Besides, how would he hold the tool and work on it at the same time?"

"Ye know better'n most that folks can beat incredible odds when they've a mind to." He smiled. "If Burt wants to keep smithin', he'll find a way to make it work."

"Easy for you to say, you have both your arms."

"One-masted ships can sail as well as two-masters, it's just a matter of the right rigging." He slid the sack off his shoulder and took the prosthesis from it. "I worked through the night to make this for him. When the time's right, I'll bring it over."

Kate inspected the stitching that secured the leather harness. "You made him a wooden arm?" Her eyes danced with awe and wonder. She smiled. "Now then, why don't you just have a seat while I get my book."

"Yer book?" he said, settling onto the seat of an ancient wooden stool.

She held up a small cloth-bound journal. "I have practically everyone in town listed in here." She opened to a random page, leaned in close so he could read along with her. "See?" she asked, pointing to the top line. "This one is Kay Greene's. The very first time she asked me to make her a dress, I jotted her measurements in here. That way, any time she wants something else, a blouse, a skirt, a coat, she doesn't have to take the time to come in for me to measure her up, because I already know the distance between her shoulders and her elbows, between her hips and her ankles."

"What if the distance around her middle should change?" he asked, grinning slyly.

"You mean if she was going to have a baby or something?"

He pictured Kay Greene. *'Tweren't no baby that puffed her belly up like a toad's throat,* he told himself, his grin growing. Eating seemed to give her the energy required to go about the "very important business" of gossiping. "Something like that."

"Well, if I should notice such a thing happening, I'd simply ask her to stop by so I could slip my tape measure around her waist." She opened the book to a blank page, slid the pencil from behind her ear and wrote John Joseph O'Keefe.

"Ye have lovely penmanship, Kate." And almost as an afterthought, he stuck on, " 'Tisn't any surprise, though; everything about ye is lovely."

She hid her blush behind a hand and took a step away.

Laying the book on the workbench, she made a tidy column along the left-hand side of J. J.'s page: Shoulders, chest, waist, biceps, shoulder-to-elbow, shoulder-to-wrist, neck-to-hips, collar, cuffs. "Now then," she began in a crisp, businesslike voice, "would you mind getting up on that box over there, so I can."

She cut herself off, and giggling, looked up at him. "Maybe you ought to stay right where you are, and I'll get on the box."

My but she's a vision, he thought. "I'll stand anywhere you tell me to." *I'll do whatever it takes to be near you.*

Kate took a cloth tape measure out of her apron pocket. If it hadn't been for the numbers, printed in bold black on the inch-wide band of material, he might not have known what it was at all. It looked more like a peculiar disk of some sort, the way she'd wound it up tight and secured it with a pin. "Why d'ye go to all the bother of wrappin' it up that way?" he asked as she unfurled it. "Wouldn't it be simpler and faster just to lay it in a drawer?"

She wrinkled her nose and shook her head. "Too messy," she said. It was all she'd needed to say, because all around him, bolts of cloth, spools of thread, needles of every size and shape, everything was arranged in an orderly fashion. Precision, he was beginning to understand, was synonymous with Kate Flynn.

Standing behind him, she held one end of the measure against a shoulder bone, unrolled the tape and pressed it against the other. "Twenty-nine," she said, and wrote the number in her book.

Quick as a bunny, she scampered round in front of him to size up the length of his arm.

"Long as I'm here," he said, "there's somethin' I feel I'm obliged to tell ye."

"Thirty-six," she said, and added it to her book. "Lift up your arms, please." When he did, she wrapped the tape measure around his chest.

Thinking she hadn't heard him, J. J. was about to repeat the statement when she scribbled "forty-eight" in her book. She wrapped the tape around his biceps. "So what have you been meaning to tell me?" she asked, writing "eighteen."

"Well," he began as she did the same to his wrist, "I don't want to worry ye, Kate, but—"

"Nine."

"But there's a good chance ye might be in danger."

She pressed the end of the tape to the front of his shoulder, and sliding the length of it between her thumb and forefinger, followed it down, stopping several inches below his hip. "We don't want your shirt coming untucked, now do we?"

He caught her wrist in a big hand. "And we don't want ye gettin' hurt, now do we?"

Kate brought in a corner of her mouth and looked into his face. The self-assured smile that had been in place the whole time she'd been measuring him disappeared when she read the stern concern in his eyes. "Well, out with it, J. J. Or would you rather see how long it takes to scare me out of my wits?"

He groaned inwardly. "Scarin' ye is the last thing I want to do."

J. J. glanced around, his gaze darting from the open door to the wide expanse of window. "Isn't there someplace we can go where we can be alone?"

Her smile gone, she gasped softly. "Why? Is the news so bad you expect me to faint dead away?"

"No."

She lifted her chin. "Then why can't you tell me here?"

He looked at the door again. "Because the wrong person might overhear."

"Adam is next door, helping Mary take inventory." The hint of a smile tugged at the corners of her mouth. "She promised to pay him in sweet treats, two pieces of candy for every hour he works."

His expression softened slightly. " 'Tisn't Adam I'm tryin' to avoid."

She bit her lower lip. "J. J.," she said, looking down, "would you mind. . . ?"

He followed her gaze to her wrist. Immediately, he released her. "Good heavens," he rasped. "Look what I've done to ye! There are likely to be welts, bruises maybe." He met her wide brown eyes, cupped her chin in a palm. "Oh, Kate, m'darlin', can ye ever forgive me?"

She seemed to pay no mind at all to the red splotches his fingers had caused on her skin. Smiling, she took the offending hand in hers and led him to the multi-cubbied shelf unit on the opposite wall, where she'd stacked bolts of material in order by weight and color. "What sort of shirt did you have in mind?" she asked, the forefinger of her free hand tapping her chin. "Cotton? Flannel?" She sent him a saucy grin. "Something a little fancier. Silk, maybe?"

What did he care what she made the shirt out of? He deserved horsehair after what he'd done to her! She was so tiny, so fragile and delicate, and she'd spent years with an abusive man. What must she think of him? "Kate," he husked, "I'm so sorry. I never meant—" Heart aching, he struggled to reclaim his former stoic demeanor. "I'd never deliberately hurt ye. I hope ye know that."

The flirty grin vanished, and in its place a warm, loving expression. "John Joseph O'Keefe," she began, "for all your size and strength, you're nothing but a big softie." Smiling tenderly, she added, "If I were a betting woman—and I'll have you know I'm not—I'd wager it gives you grief to squash a bug under your boot." She pressed a palm to his cheek. "Don't ask me how, but I'm as sure as sure can be that you'd never hurt me, not in any way." Taking his hand, Kate wrapped it around her wrist, the same wrist he'd squeezed moments ago, and stroked his fingers. "You're upset about something, very upset. Now why don't you tell me what dangers lurk in my future, so we can put this little incident behind us?"

This wasn't the first time he'd had to force himself to resist the urge to wrap his arms around her, hold her so close that not so much as a breath of air could pass between them. J. J. suspected it was far from the last time, either. "Might we find a less conspicuous place?"

She patted his hand. "Of course. We'll go upstairs, have a cup of tea." She glanced at the clock. "It's nearly noon. I'll fix you a sandwich." Without turning loose of his hand, Kate headed for the staircase. "I baked a ham yesterday. Sweet potatoes, butter beans, biscuits." Laughing, she started up the steps. "You'd think I was cooking for an army, instead of—"

He'd come here to warn her to be careful, expecting that, once he spelled out his worst fears, she might need a bit of comfort and reassurance. How had things gotten so turned around, he wondered, that she was offering comfort to him instead?

Overcome with emotion, he gently tugged her hand, and when she turned to see why he'd stopped her, J. J. said, "There's somethin' mighty peculiar goin' on inside of me, Kate Flynn. I might as well tell ye that right up front. If the truth be told, I don't know what to make of it, but—"

Even standing a step higher than J. J., she had to look up a bit to meet his eyes. A corner of her mouth lifted in the beginnings of a smile. "Maybe you got hold of some rancid meat at the fair yesterday."

He grinned. Spoiled food had absolutely nothing to do with the sensation roiling in his gut. The urge to hug her gave way to an incredible yearning to kiss her. *Patience, man,* he cautioned, gritting his teeth. *There's a time and place for everything; this is neither the time nor the place for. . .*

She leaned forward suddenly and, standing on tip-toe, pressed her lips to his forehead. "Well," she said matter-of-factly, "you don't have a fever, you'll be happy to know."

"Fever?" he repeated, his voice froggy with emotion. He cleared his throat.

"Must be something else that's bothering your stomach."

'Tisn't my stomach that's upset now! he thought, grinning wryly.

She continued to chatter the whole way upstairs. "I know tradition dictates that we hold a palm against the face to test for fever. But the lips, the lips are the best way I know to take a person's temperature." On the landing, she stopped, tilted her head slightly. "Because the lips, you see, are so much more sensitive to heat than the hands. And speaking of hands." She pulled him into the kitchen and stood him beside a chair. "Why don't you wash yours while I heat up the water."

She put the kettle on to boil, sliced bread and ham and cheese, built him a three-inch thick sandwich, and sat a wedge of apple pie on the table. "How do you like your tea," she asked, "with cream and sugar?"

"No. I prefer it plain." He raised a brow. "My tea, that is."

She lay the sandwich on a plate, cut it in half, placed it in front of him. And tucking a napkin into his collar, she said, "There's more where that came from, so don't be shy."

As Kate sat across from him and spooned a teaspoon of sugar into her cup, J. J. hoped she couldn't hear his stomach rumbling. He hadn't eaten since supper the night before, and the food made his mouth water.

Her spoon made quiet, clinking sounds against the china. "Are you testing me, J. J.?"

"Testing you?" He picked up the sandwich.

"To see how patient I am."

He sent her an "I don't understand" expression.

"You didn't come here because you needed a shirt."

One cheek puffed full of ham and bread, he stopped chewing.

Resting her elbows on the table, she folded both hands beneath her chin. "And you aren't here for the free food."

He put the sandwich down, wiped his hands on the linen napkin she'd sat beside his plate. "Maybe I stopped by because I enjoy yer company. Did ye ever consider that, Kate?"

Again, she answered his question with another: "Why don't

you just spit it out?"

He combed his fingers through his hair. "What do you know about what happened to the people who lived in this house?"

"That there was a fire, and they were trapped inside."

"And do ye know how the fire was started?"

"Thaddius thinks a lantern must have overturned, because Mary smelled whale oil just before. But what does any of that have to do with me? I didn't even buy the house 'til. . ." She sipped her tea. "The house had been empty more than a year when Adam and I moved in. It took me nearly two years more to make it livable."

He remembered how, soon after settling in Currituck, he'd sometimes see her as he passed by, busily scraping, scrubbing, painting.

"Didn't ye think it odd there was so little damage downstairs?"

She inclined her head. "Why, yes, as a matter of fact, I have wondered about that."

"I'm rememberin' an earlier conversation of ours, when you said you didn't like it when folks beat 'round the bush."

"That's right. 'Say what you mean, and mean what you say,' that's my motto."

"Then I'll get right to the point." He swallowed, then said, " 'Twasn't an accident, Kate."

"What do you mean, it wasn't an accident. Of course it was. Thaddius said. . ."

"Whale oil was the fuel, all right, but it didn't come from any tilted lamp. Someone doused the place with the stuff, then threw the bolt at the top of the stairs. They'd likely have survived if they'd been able to get out."

She gasped. "How horrible!" Then, in a soft, small voice, "Who would do such a thing?" And a second later, "How do you know so much about it?"

"I talked with Ernie Walters."

"Why would you go to him about a fire that happened here, years before you moved to town?"

"Because," he said, taking her hand, "I've learned there's a chance history might repeat itself."

She stared, openmouthed, for a long moment. "But why, J. J.?"

She's some kind of woman, he thought. Just look at her, sittin' there, tryin' so hard to be brave. When Adam had first told him what Bobby planned to do, he didn't give a hang if the boy was barely thirteen years old, he'd wanted to wring the hoodlum's neck. But a quick walk on the dock had cleared his head, calmed him down. "Violence begets violence," he'd told himself. There were better ways, gentler ways to deal with Bobby.

But now, seeing the fear and misery written on Kate's lovely face, J. J. found himself fighting the murderous urges again. She should be smiling, happy, at peace, not wringing her hands and biting her lips, worrying about her safety and her son's. He wanted to throttle anyone who got in the way of her serenity, who threatened her security. If Bobby thought himself man enough to think up such a dastardly thing, and old enough to carry out the evil deed, he was old enough to be punished like a man for his crimes.

And J. J. was just the man to do the punishing.

He shoved the sandwich plate aside. "Sorry to put you to the bother, Kate," he said, shoving his chair back. "Guess I'm not as hungry as I thought."

She sent him a trembling smile. Under other circumstances, she would have said, "Don't worry, it was no bother." If she hadn't been trying so hard not to cry, she might have told him, "I'll just wrap the sandwich in a tea towel, save it for Adam's lunch."

But she hadn't spoken, hadn't stood when he did him, hadn't walked him to the door the way she had last time they had shared a cup of tea. Fear had frozen her to her chair, he knew, and years of having to fend for herself had made her try to hide it.

He wanted to take her in his arms and whisper words of comfort and assurance into her ears. He started to tell her not to worry, that things would be all right, that he'd make them all right! But a sob ached in his throat as his fists opened and closed at his sides. How could such feelings of tenderness be simmering in his heart while vengeful, boiling bloodlust coursed through his veins?

He left without giving her that promise, without telling her good-bye, without so much as thanking her for the tea. His boots thundered down the wooden steps, his heart hammered against his ribs.

Ye might never be lucky enough to call her yer own, John Joseph O'Keefe, but ye'll do yer level best to see she that she's safe.

And if that meant eliminating the reason she was afraid, so be it.

❧

"Where are you headed in such an all-fired hurry?"

"Step out of the way," J. J. cautioned. "I've business to attend to."

Despite the angry warning, Ernie Walters blocked his path. "What kind of business?" Crossing both arms over his chest, he frowned, tilting his head back and regarding J. J. through his narrow, gold-rimmed spectacles.

He tried to side-step the man. "It's none of your concern."

"I've been a sheriff nearly as long as you've been alive, O'Keefe; I know trouble when I see it, and there's trouble written all over your face."

J. J. said through clenched teeth, "I'm askin' ye polite as I know how, Ernie, let me by."

"You headed over to the boy's place?"

J. J. ground his molars together. And though he already knew the answer, he asked, "What boy?"

"Back off, O'Keefe. There's no evidence linking Bobby to any crime."

"Evidence! There are dead pets and terrified women all over town. Now, some might consider killin' cats and stealin' purses nothin' more than childhood pranks, but I don't. And even for those who don't find his behavior intolerable, burnin' down houses with folks still in 'em—"

"Like I said, O'Keefe," the sheriff interrupted calm as you please, "there's no proof he had anything to do with that, so back off."

J. J.'s forefinger popped from his fist as if fired from a pistol. "You're the man with the badge," he steamed, poking the finger into Walters' chest. "Tell me you're doin' somethin' to get that ruffian under control. Then I'll back off, and not a minute sooner."

The sheriff gave the offending finger a casual glance. "I could haul you off to jail right now, if I had a mind to."

"On what charges!"

"Assaulting an officer of the law for starters."

This wasn't solving anything. While he and Walters stood toe-to-toe, J. J. realized, Bobby could be off doing only God knew what!

He pocketed his hands and decided to take another tack. "Sorry," he muttered, slowly shaking his head. "I don't know how you stomach police work, Ernie. Ye're a better man than me, that's for sure, keepin' yer temper in check whilst criminals like Bobby get away with murder."

Walters eyed him suspiciously for a moment. "What-say we start this conversation over, from the beginning?"

J. J. nodded agreeably.

"So tell me, O'Keefe, where are you headed in such an all-fired hurry?"

He took a deep breath. "To me warehouse," he fibbed. "I've got a boat to build for a big shot Virginia banker."

With a one-fingered salute, the sheriff sauntered on down

the walkway. "Have yourself a fine day, O'Keefe," he said over his shoulder.

"And you do the same, Sheriff."

J. J. felt the mighty hand of God had affected this little scene. Being stopped by the sheriff had probably saved him from doing something he'd regret for the rest of his life. *Thank Ye, Lord,* he prayed, *for bein' on me side and at me side.*

" 'Vengeance is mine; I will repay, saith the Lord,' " he quoted. If there was an ounce of truth in the verse, J. J. believed Bobby was in for a rude awakening

And soon.

❧

"What're you doing, Adam?"

The boy knew without looking up from his work who had asked the question. He took a deep breath and rolled his eyes. "What does it look like I'm doing, Phoebe?"

"I dunno," she sing-songed.

Despite himself, Adam peered over his shoulder just as she daintily ground the toe of her boot into the dirt and chewed the tip of one blonde braid.

"Are you building a raft?"

He sat back on his heels and looked at his creation. Logs of this size were scarce in Currituck. It had taken a week to gather enough wood for his project. And then there had been the matter of lashing them together. He'd spent two days braiding scraps of twine picked from the trash bin behind the Crofton's store, and a week tying together the odd-sized pieces of hemp he'd found here and there.

Phoebe wrinkled her nose at the mast. "Aren't you afraid it'll fall over?"

"Fall over? Ha! There are enough pegs in that thing to sink a battleship."

And it was true. He'd found hundreds of old, rusty nails in a wooden barrel behind Mr. Roberts' shop. The carpenter had no use for them, and gladly let Adam haul them away. There were perhaps two dozen straight ones in the bunch, but most were bent, and some had no heads. One by one, Adam lay the nails on a flat boulder and hammered them into submission.

The mast itself was constructed of two unwieldy limbs, laid out in the shape of a cross and tethered with his best piece of rope. It hadn't been easy, standing the thing up, but he'd managed, miraculously, to wedge it into the tight round hole he'd sawed into the center of the raft. There was still a slight play in the fit, but he'd learned by watching J. J. that with time all wood swells to make a tight fit. His easiest task so far had been the sail. He'd seen a picture of a Viking longboat in one of his mother's books, and patterned his sail after the Norsemen's. Once, it had been a blanket on his bed. Now, held to the wood by dozens of nails, it caught the gentle east-northeast wind and set the mast to creaking, squeaking, straining against its rope tethers with every slight turn.

Trouble was, the whole thing had teetered and tottered and threatened to topple with the first good puff of air. That's when the nails really came in handy. Using every scrap of lumber he could wheedle out of Mr. Roberts, he secured them at forty-five degree angle—all fifteen of them—between the mast and the raft floor. There were four nails left over when he was finished, so he'd banged them in, too, just for good measure.

Blinking flirtatiously, Phoebe asked, "Where are you going, Adam?"

"Across the sound."

"Does your mother know?"

" 'Course she does," he fibbed. "I told her I'd be leavin', soon as I get the thing built."

Her round, blue eyes widened with adulation, and her voice took on a whispery, reverent tone. "You mean, you didn't have to ask permission?"

His chest and chin jutted out, he said, "I know what I'm

doin'. I don't need permission."

She looked toward the sound. "But why are you going there? There's nothing but sand and—"

Adam stood and faced seaward. "Have you been there?"

She pouted prettily. "No."

"Then how do you know what's there?"

A little shrug was her answer.

"Just maybe there are diamonds in the rocks. Maybe there's a gold mine. Maybe a pirate treasure trunk has washed up on. . ."

"And maybe," Phoebe giggled, "you're a silly old boy who reads too many novels."

"Novels? I don't even like to read my speller," he countered, dropping to his knees. "I think I hear your mother calling," he added, tugging at a rope.

"You're just trying to get rid of me again."

"If I thought it'd work," he said dully, "I'd tell you Santa Claus was calling."

From the corner of his eye, he saw her lower lip poke out in a pretty pout. Just as quickly, Phoebe brightened. "Can I help?" she asked sweetly.

"There's nothin' for you to do."

"I could make you sandwiches and bake you cookies, to take with you on your trip. I could put them all into a jar, with a nice tight lid, so they'd stay dry. I could."

Actually, that didn't sound half bad. "Will you make the sandwiches yourself?"

She grabbed hold of the outer corners of her skirt, held it out until it formed a semicircle. "Any simpleton can pile meat and bread together," she said, giggling. "Why, I'll bet even you could do it, Adam Flynn!"

He shook his head. *Girls,* he grumped. "What about the cookies?"

"What's your favorite," she wanted to know, "shortbread cookies or oatmeal?"

His mouth began to water. Licking his lips, Adam said, "I guess I'll leave that up to you. You'd better get baking now, though, 'cause I'll be leaving tomorrow."

"But Adam," she said, looking up, "there's a storm coming. I heard my grandfather say the last time the sky looked this way, a williwaw blew through here."

"Aw, a little rain never hurt anybody," he laughed.

"Have you ever heard about what a williwaw can do?"

"Can't say that I have."

"Why, they can blow whole towns away. Just think what a storm like that could do to your rickety, little raft."

He frowned. "Rickety? My raft ain't rickety."

She frowned right back. "Well, it won't hold up in a williwaw. You'd better wait 'til the storm passes to take your trip."

"You ain't my ma, Phoebe. I'm goin', and that's that."

Sighing, she rolled her eyes. "Well, it's your life."

"That's right, it is," he said to her back.

Despite his bravado, Adam looked at the angry, darkening skies overhead, and shivered.

❧

J. J., hunched over his forge, pumped the bellows to increase the heat. The lump of iron he held in his tongs glowed bright cherry-red as he lay it on his anvil to pound it into the shape of a cleat. From the corner of his eye, he noticed Bobby Banks loitering near the door, and he had an idea.

"Hey, there, lad; come on in!"

The boy swaggered deeper into the warehouse, hands pocketed, touching everything in sight with his narrow-eyed gaze. He stopped a few feet shy of the forge. "What's that you're makin'?"

J. J. shoved the cleat back into the coals, tromped on the bellows pedal again. Flames leapt up, licked the underside of the cleat and his tongs as well.

"Looks mighty hot," Bobby observed.

J. J. gave the iron cleat a few, last ping-pinging whacks of his hammer. It had to be smoothly well-rounded if a sailor's knot was to slip on and off easily. Most folks squinted when they got this near the fiery intensity of J. J.'s forge, for it threatened to singe the skin and blind the eyes. Not Bobby Banks. He seemed rooted to the spot, lips slightly parted, breathing heavily, mesmerized by the glare.

"Don't stare at it, lad," J. J. scolded, "it'll strike ye sightless, sure."

Blinking, the boy roused himself from his self-induced daze. He licked his lips. Swallowed. "Looks mighty hot," he ground out.

"Don't you worry. I know how to put out a fire."

Bobby met J. J.'s eyes. "How?"

Sneering, he said, "Ye drown it." He punctuated his answer by driving the fire-red tongs, cleat and all, into an iron-banded wooden bucket, and held it there. It spattered, sputtered, hissed like the call of a giant turbid snake, creating a billowing plume of thick, snow-white smoke that, for a moment, blotted Bobby from view. It took no more than an instant for the spume to fizzle as the cleat cooled, more than long enough. Bobby had gotten J. J.'s point, as evidenced by the frightened-turned-fearsome expression on the boy's face.

J. J. had never seen such raw, unbridled hate, not even in the most cold-blooded English landlord. This man-sized boy had not yet lived fifteen years, yet loathing that seemed to have no particular source, no particular target, burned hotter in his eyes than the cleat had burned in the forge. What had fueled his malevolent, baleful maliciousness?

This was a dark and dangerous being, villainous to its core. He'd never looked into the eyes of evil before, but he was looking at it now, and it shook J. J. to his core.

seven

He'd seen a few storms, some of them serious, but nothing to compare with this one.

You should have listened to Phoebe, and waited for it to pass. Adam frowned. *But since when have you listened to any old girl?*

He'd left at dawn, thinking the ominous gray skies overhead meant nothing more serious than a few lightning strikes, some thunder, maybe a gust of wind or two. But this!

The sucking undertow of great crashing waves drove him farther, farther from shore, and he lifted his head, squinted past the stinging raindrops pelting his face. *If I could just get a glimpse of the dock,* he thought, *maybe I could steer myself back.*

The raft was the only thing between him and death. He was glad he'd spent as much time as he had, constructing it; glad he'd connected each log to the other carefully, with sturdy hemp. But how long would the knots of those mis-matched pieces stay together? How many more jolts could they endure before snapping?

"If a job's worth doing, it's worth doing well." He hadn't taken J. J.'s advice seriously at the time, but right now it seemed like the most important lesson he'd ever learned, and he was glad he'd taken it to heart.

Adam gripped his lifeline tighter. He'd never been more afraid for his life. Not when J. J. was chasing him through the streets of Currituck, not even when he looked up into Bobby's angry face.

Yes, he'd survived ordinary storms before.

But this was no ordinary storm.

He had sensed distant danger when he'd set sail at dawn. Something told him to turn around, to take this trip another day. But the adventure of it—and the fact that he'd stupidly bragged to Phoebe the he was going—spurred him on.

Now, one cheek pressed hard against the rough bark deck of his raft, Adam held his breath as yet another wave crashed over him. *Thank You,* he prayed when it didn't wash him overboard, *and thank You for giving me the good sense to lash my supplies down before leaving.*

The craft rose on a hissing, spitting wave. Lightning exploded behind the tattered gray clouds. A powerful thunderclap vibrated his bones. *Dear God,* he whimpered, closing his eyes, *please help me get back home. Help me get—*

The angry sea surged yet again, lifting him and the tiny boat higher, higher, until he could see nothing but smoky sky all around him. The ropes that held the raft together creaked and groaned. Yes, he'd done his all-out best, and built it well—but well enough to stand up to a beating like this?

The watery world all around him became in his terrified mind a monstrous, living creature, gurgling and growling as sea swells surged up the beast's muscular arms. Waves curled like powerful fists and pounded down with the force and fury of a giant. The Atlantic was Goliath, and Adam was David. But unlike David, Adam had no weapon to hurl in self defense, nothing to protect himself against the power of the sea.

If you'd listened to Phoebe, he thought again, *you'd be home now, safe and sound, warm and dry.*

But it had seemed like such a short distance across the sound. Convinced he could travel over the water in no time, he had decided to take the chance he'd make it to land before the rains began. *So much for outwitting nature!* he scolded himself.

Every now and again, the storm calmed a bit, and for fleeting moments, Adam could see the shore, J. J.'s warehouse,

the roof of his mother's dress shop, other stores tucked along
Currituck's Main Street, their chimneys poking up from the
horizon reminding him of the hats that lined the shelves of
Mr. Gentry's menswear store.

If I make it back in one piece, he promised God, *I'll never
miss Sunday school again.*

Phoebe had repeated her grandfather's prediction that a
williwaw was on its way, and Adam had poked fun at the old
man's name for a hurricane. In his eight and three quarters
years, he'd never seen one, but he'd heard plenty about the
flood waters that drowned everything in their paths. J. J. had
said. "It's the winds that scare sailors," he explained. "All
over the world, they have strange names for the mighty
winds. They call 'em 'levanters' in the Orient. In Africa, 'har-
mattan,' and 'simoom' in the Middle East. Whatever they call
'em, they're wild and violent and bent on destruction."

Could this be a hurricane? Adam wondered.

He could only hope and pray it was not, for if the tales J. J.
had told about these vicious storms were true, he was
doomed.

If he died, who would fetch wood for his mother's stove?
Who would carry her groceries? Who would help her wrap
cloth around wooden blocks?

Adam pictured her, wind mussing her hair as she stood at
the door, a shawl pulled tight around her shoulders, watching
with worried eyes for her only boy's safe return.

Lying on his stomach, Adam pressed his face into his forearms and struggled to blink back hot tears. *One thing you
don't need right now is more water in your eyes! Besides,* he
reminded himself, he'd be nine on his next birthday. *You're
too old to cry. Too old to cry.*

Still the tears came, because he was afraid. More afraid
than he'd ever been. Adam didn't want to die. If he had to
meet his Maker, he could think of far better ways to do it than
by drowning during a gale!

The ugly truth was, he had no one but himself to blame for his predicament. He went from listing "ifs" to listing "maybes."

If he'd listened to Phoebe, if he'd asked his mother's permission, if he'd at least told someone where he was headed they might have tried to talk him out of the trip. If any of those things had happened. . .

Maybe he wouldn't be riding the wild waves now. Maybe he wouldn't be scared out of his skin. Maybe his mother wouldn't be worrying. He had no choice but to lie still and wait it out, and hope the angry sea would soon tire of toying with him.

It was surprisingly cold for a summer day. And he was surprisingly tired for a boy of not-quite nine. Tired of holding fast to the ropes that kept him from being eaten alive by the hungry waves, tired of holding his breath as the waves pummeled him, tired of worrying which gust, which wave would be the end of him.

He'd likely swallowed a gallon of the Atlantic's salty water, and his sickened stomach churned now, like the swollen sea. He yawned, downing yet another mouthful of the briny liquid. If he was exhausted enough to yawn, could sleep be far behind?

Stay awake, he warned, *or you'll end up fish food for sure!*

Just then, he spied the end of the rope he planned to use to tether the raft once he reached dry land. Flat on his stomach, he crawled toward the craft's far corner. "Thank You, Lord!" he said through clenched teeth, pulling the six feet of excess hemp from the water. "More than enough to tie myself to the deck."

Adam wrapped it tight around his middle, threaded the end through the loops that were holding the logs together, and breathed a sigh of relief. Now, at least, he had a chance to make it. Now, he might not be gobbled up by the hungry sea should fatigue overtake him before he made it home again.

Home.

It was a mistake to look toward shore. Adam's heart sank for the riptide had pushed him miles away. The storm had a life of its own, had become a villainous entity that kidnapped and held him for ransom, far out to sea. Miles from his mother, miles from his warm, dry bed, miles from—

Between the wind and the waves, you'll never make it back alive!

His short trip across the sound had likely cost him his life. The storm had won.

But not before he gave it one last try.

Adam never went anywhere without his pencil, and dug around for it in his sack. He'd learned in school that the ancients had written with chunks of chalk and rock. Medieval monks, like the Egyptians before them, made their marks using metallic lead. "It's nothing short of a miracle," Miss Henderson had said during the lesson, "that a few centuries ago, to keep his hands clean, someone decided to encase the graphite in wood."

Now if only he had something to write on. But what could there possibly be on this drenched, soaked raft?

Adam hatched an idea.

He'd built the raft, partly of birch logs. But he hadn't peeled them. The rain and the waves had caused them to swell, and their bark to lift. Carefully, Adam peeled a chunk of bark from one.

"Please, Lord," he prayed, "let it work."

Dear Ma, he wrote, thanking God that the letters were, indeed, adhering to the pulpy underside of the bark, *I'm sorry I didn't tell you what I was up to, because it looks like I'll meet my Maker today. Remember me now and then. I'll think of you, too. Your son, Adam Flynn.*

Carefully, Adam rolled the bark like a scroll, and stuffed it into a jar and jammed the cork into place as tightly as his wet hands would allow. For a moment, he clutched it to his chest, and prayed that God would carry it to his mother.

His mother.

Oh, how he'd miss her! He wished he'd taken the time to give her one last hug before sneaking off this morning.

Yawning again, he tossed the jar into the water. It bobbled, tumbled, rolled upside down and right-side up again before disappearing into the froth.

ঌ

"Oh, J. J.," Kate cried, "will he ever wake up?"

He wanted to give her an answer that would comfort and reassure her. But Adam had been unconscious for nearly twelve hours.

"The longer a person remains in this state," Doctor Peterson said, "the less likely he'll come out of it."

A moment of silence ticked by before Kate found her voice. "Nonsense! He's a strong, healthy boy. He's going to be fine. You'll see."

J. J. watched her with careful eyes. Kate perched on the edge of Adam's bed, alternately laying cool compresses on his bruised forehead and running fingers through his hair. She hadn't left his side since J. J. had carried the boy up the stairs, and the signs of exhaustion and worry were evident on her pretty face.

"Kate," J. J. said softly, one hand on her shoulder, "let me take over for a while. Have a bite to eat, get some rest. Do it for Adam, if not for yerself."

She never took her eyes off the boy. "I can't, J. J. I have to be here when he wakes up."

"You've got to get some food into your stomach," the doctor argued, pocketing his stethoscope. "J. J.'s right. You'll be useless to Adam if you fall over in a dead faint."

She shook her head. "I'll eat and sleep when I know he's out of danger," she insisted without looking up.

Doc Peterson and J. J. exchanged worried glances. "I have several more patients to see yet this evening. That storm did a lot more damage than the last one."

J. J. pictured Currituck, its usually clean streets muddied, littered with soggy newspaper pages, chunks of wood, tin cans half-filled with murky rainwater. Several houses had been completely destroyed. The porches of others had been torn away. The entire backside of the church was missing. Many of the headstones in the graveyard beside it lay like wounded soldiers in the muck, and the tidy white fence that had once surrounded the cemetery had been disassembled, board by board.

The little row of buildings where his warehouse stood had been miraculously spared. Though the wind had torn a door from the hinges of his warehouse, and he'd have to replace several shingles, all in all, his home and place of business had been untouched. He thought it odd, the way the brutal blasts had blown the dock away yet left the boat he'd berthed in the harbor in perfect condition.

Though they knew the storm was coming, the severity of it caught the townsfolk unawares, for it hit its zenith at high tide, magnifying the effects of the nor'easter.

Yes, Doc Peterson would have more patients to see tonight. He'd be busy for days, J. J. knew, splinting broken bones, stitching up wounds, patting pumice onto the bruises and abrasions of survivors.

Roberts, the carpenter, had asked J. J. to lend a hand in constructing coffins, six to be exact, for those who hadn't been so lucky. He ought to be getting to work on them, but he didn't want to leave Kate just yet.

"See that she has something to eat," the doctor instructed as he packed up his medical bag. "And please, get her to lie down before she falls down."

"I'll try, but ye know Kate."

Doc Peterson glanced at her. "Well," he said on an exhausted sigh, "do your best."

When he was gone, J. J. slid an arm around Kate's shoulders.

She didn't even seem to notice. His heart ached for her. She had no one in this world but her son. If something happened to him—

J. J. preferred not to dwell on Kate's state of mind should the boy take a turn for the worse. He walked into the kitchen, set a kettle of water to boiling, and rounded up enough ingredients to make up some soup. *Maybe the scent of onions and ham will rouse her,* he hoped. *But even if it doesn't, she'll be eatin' it when it's cooked, and that's that.*

Meanwhile, he brewed her a cup of tea, stirred in a spoonful of honey, and placed it on the table beside Adam's bed. When it cooled down some, he'd hold it to her lips and make her drink if he had to.

He sat beside her again and wrapped her in his arms. "Ah, Kate, m'darlin'," he said, pulling her close, "ye're tremblin' like the last leaf of autumn."

She melted against him like butter on a hot biscuit. "I've never been more frightened in all my life," she admitted in a small, whispery voice. "He looks so young, so helpless lying there all bandaged up that way."

J. J. rubbed soothing circles on her narrow back. "I know," he said softly. "I know."

But it was a lie. *What d'ye know about the love of a mother for her child?* Oh, he'd known many kinds and depths of love—for his family, his work, Ireland, Kate. But at this moment, as the Dark Fairy hovered near her door, he could only imagine what it might be like to love in that all consuming, unconditional way, and wonder if—

She sat back, took his face in her hands. "If it hadn't been for you."

He could see how hard she was trying to keep her emotions under control.

"He would have died for sure if—"

He watched her bite her lower lip in an attempt to stanch a sob.

"But thanks to you, he has a chance." Resting her cheek against his chest, Kate added, "How does it feel to be a hero, J. J.?"

Hero? Him? "I wouldn't know."

"You saved his life."

He winced. "I did what any man would have done under the circumstances."

She shook her head. "I don't believe that. Not for a minute. 'Any man' wouldn't have risked his own skin to save a boy from drowning."

"But of course he would."

She held a silencing finger in the air. "But nothing! There's no sense denying it. Doc Peterson saw the whole thing from his window. He said you put yourself in danger, jumping into the water the way you did. Said if the winds didn't get you, he was sure the waves would, and that—"

"He said too much," J. J. protested. "Now, why don't ye have a sip of the tea I made for ye? I stirred in a spoonful of honey, just the way ye like it."

He felt Kate stiffen slightly.

It started quiet and slow, like the distant, plaintive lament of a lone wolf, not a moan exactly, but not a cry, either. It was a sad, sorrowful sound, reminiscent of those dreadful days in Ireland, when his sister Erin lay dying and his mother, too weak herself to comfort her, grieved, helpless to save that nearly-grown child of her womb.

Kate's shoulders lurched twice, three times at most, and then she froze, holding her breath, clutching at a wrinkle in his shirt. J. J. felt her warm tears against his skin and wanted to sob himself. He hadn't known how to soothe his own heart-broken mother; how did he hope to relieve Kate's utter sadness? He could easily heft huge logs, stand them upright once he'd hewn them into masts. But what good was his physical prowess, when he was powerless to offer Kate the smallest solace? He'd filled his journal with words that painted pictures, set scenes, made moods, yet he couldn't think of a single thing to say to give her peace and some respite from her tribulations.

And so he simply held her, tenderly, big hands gently stroking her back and shoulders, and hoped the love in his heart would radiate from him to her by way of his fingertips, soothing her, easing her fears.

Some minutes later, her sobs subsided. "I'm sorry, J. J.," came her ragged sigh.

"Sorry?" A joyless chuckle crackled from his throat. "Whatever for?"

"I've gotten your shirt all wet."

A feeling surged over him, a sensation that reminded him of the tales told by Irish sailors about the tranquil, tepid waters of the southseas, waters that foamed and frothed over a man like gentle hands; soft, sultry winds that ruffled and fluttered like the whispering wings of angels. He wanted, needed to define the sensation, give it a name. A millisecond, perhaps less, passed before a word came to mind.

Love.

Deep, abiding, overwhelming, it made him feel helpless and Herculean at one and the same time: Weak, because for all his muscular might, he did not have the haleness to fight it; strong, because he knew it would enable him to endure any hardship, any pain. His body might well live on without it, but his heart and soul would not.

Love.

Or Kate? J. J. didn't know where one began and the other left off. In his heart, in his head, they were synonymous.

"Good thing it's summertime," she said, her breath warming his chest, "you could catch a chill, walking around in a wet shirt."

Nothin' can chill me, he told himself, *not the wicked winds of winter, not snow from the mountaintops, not the icy blasts of the northlands; I'll always be warm, as long as ye're near me.*

Kate sighed dreamily, snuggled closer. "Why, J. J., that's the most beautiful thing anyone has ever said to me."

Either she could read his mind, or he'd said aloud the words stamped onto his soul. He looked into her face, into eyes so round and brown, he likened it to staring into a pond at midnight, when the moon dipped low in the sky and kissed the rippling ebbtides that danced at the shoreline with shimmering, silvery light.

Ah, Kate, m'darlin', he thought, *I could live out the rest of me days, lookin' into yer lovely eyes, because I love ye with all that I am, and all that I'll ever be.*

She sat up, dried those lovely eyes on the hem of her apron, and straightened her back. "You have the heart of a poet, John Joseph O'Keefe," she said, forcing a brave smile.

Had he spoken his thoughts aloud again? Or had she read his mind once more, as he'd so often suspected she had?

She reached for the teacup, sipped daintily. It made a glassy *rat-a-tat-tat* against the saucer balanced on her trembling palm. "Sweetened to perfection, just as you promised."

If only he could promise that Adam would wake up, that when he did, he'd be his usual, robust and rowdy self. If only he could promise a fortune-filled future, a life free from everyday frustrations. He wanted to give her security. Surround her with safety. Shroud her with happiness. Because she deserved all that and more.

Suddenly, J. J. was painfully aware how very little he had to offer her—a huge and hulking warehouse, filled with halfbuilt ships and bottomless boats; two rooms above it, empty, save a narrow, creaking cot and a rickety table and chairs; a history of violence, earned courtesy of the Marquis of Queensbury.

"Adam looks so peaceful, lying there, doesn't he?" she whispered, taking J. J.'s hand.

He nodded, giving hers a gentle squeeze.

"He wouldn't look that way if he were in any pain." She

met his eyes. "Would he?"

J. J. read the hope, the expectation shining in those wide, innocent orbs. "He's restin' easy, Kate," he husked. "And so should you be. Ye're lookin' a mite pale."

Kate waved his concern away. "Oh," she sighed, "but life can be hard, can't it?"

"It can, but it's a mite easier to bear, when ye have—when ye have a friend to lean on."

Kate put the cup and saucer back on the nightstand. "Please don't say that."

Her voice was so soft, her eyes so sad. "Don't say what?"

Long lashes dusted her cheeks as she looked down at her hand, resting lightly upon his knee. "Don't say you're just a friend. You're much, much more than that."

Could she possibly mean—? Because if she did, his world would be—

His heart thrummed, each hard-beating throb more emboldening than the last as he took her face in his hands. "I'm nothin' but a thick-headed Irishman, Kate," he said, eyes blazing into hers. "I'm afraid I have to ask ye to explain."

With a smile of admiration, appreciation, adoration, she said, "How you're more than a friend, you mean?"

J. J. nodded. Would she say it? Or should he? Dare he admit that he was hopelessly, endlessly in love with her?

She began haltingly, "I think. I think maybe I've fallen—"

"Oh, why don't you just kiss her, J. J.?"

Stunned into silent shock, they focused on the boy's storm-battered face.

Kate wrapped her son in a hearty hug. "Adam," she cried, gently kissing his cheeks, his forehead, the tip of his nose, "you're all right. You're all right!"

"No, I'm not," he protested, holding up a hand to fend off motherly ministrations. He locked onto J. J.'s gray gaze. "Don't just stand there, J. J.," he pleaded, his customary teasing grin back in place, "make her stop before she smothers me to death."

Swallowing a sob of relief, J. J. lay a hand on the boy's shoulder, gave it a fatherly squeeze. "I'll not stop her, lad. She's earned every smooch, worryin' over ye as she has since I pulled ye out of the drink. If the storm didn't kill ye, surely a few kisses won't hurt ye none." He paused, cocked an eyebrow, and added, "Consider yerself lucky she's not smackin' the cheeks ye sit upon instead. Ye deserve it, after all, sailin' off into the eye of a storm like ye did, without a word to anybody."

When Kate turned to face him, he half expected her to scold him for chastising Adam. Instead, what he read in her tear-shimmering eyes set his heart to pumping with relief, and joy, and expectation.

She loves ye, he realized. *Kate Flynn loves ye!*

ॐ

Bobby Banks loved it when a plan came together.

It was long past dusk when he sauntered down the street, hands in his pockets and whistling "The Riflemen of Bennington." An appropriate tune, he thought, since O'Keefe hailed from the British Isles.

He'd never much cared for the Irishman, a fact that had little or nothing to do with the way he'd pulverized his father in the ring. Bobby didn't like any man who seemed able to know his thoughts, and O'Keefe appeared to be a master at that particular talent. Still, he could have taken the man or not.

Until lately.

That all changed a couple days back, when, as was his custom, he'd been prowling around town looking for something to do, someone to do it to. He's stopped in the warehouse doorway, watched O'Keefe hammering a misshapen lump of iron into a cleat that would one day hold fast a ship's line. He'd been in the workshop before, many times, but never when the Irishman was about. That day, the owner had actually invited him inside.

He should have suspected something was afoot.

The friendly greeting quickly turned ominous, and Bobby hadn't understood why the ex-boxer had aimed that gray-eyed glare at him, nor why his lip had curled with disgust. But he had no trouble comprehending what the man had said. Well, not so much what he'd said as what his words had implied: O'Keefe had made it painfully clear that he knew what happened to the Norris family all those years ago.

There was only one way he could know. That mealy-mouthed blabbermouth Adam Flynn had told him about the threat.

He despised Adam. *Little squirt made me look bad in front of the boys,* he fumed, narrowing his eyes. Adam had blatantly disobeyed a direct order by not delivering that journal. Worse, he'd seemed downright pleased to have announced his insubordination for everyone to hear. No boy had ever stood up to him that way before, least of all a twit half his size!

Clenching his jaw, Bobby ground his fists deeper into his pockets. *The little snot is gonna pay for crossin' me.*

The mutinous act turned out to be—what did the grown-ups call it?—a blessing in disguise. Bobby hadn't needed the journal after all, because he'd devised a new scheme. One that would hurt O'Keefe worse than anything folks could say about him because of the contents of that stupid book.

And he hadn't needed to burn down Kate Flynn's dress shop, either. *First of all, it's exactly what the brat is expectin'.*

With this plan, you can kill two birdbrains with one stone, he thought, grinning at his clever rewriting of the tired old cliché.

He'd been watching O'Keefe for days now, and knew even before the man climbed the stairs that he would leave the coals glowing in the forge. Whether he did so because he forgot to douse them or because red-hot briquettes would fire faster in the morning, Bobby didn't care.

Long as they're hot coals, that's all that matters.

He knew where O'Keefe kept his coal scuttle, where to find the short-handled shovel to scoop out the embers. And the moment the Irishman was out of sight, Bobby slipped in through a back window propped open earlier with a twig, and headed straight for the forge.

Holding his breath, he winced, fearing O'Keefe might have heard the loud scrape of the coal shovel as it dug to the bottom of the forge. Satisfied he had not, Bobby filled the tin scuttle to the halfway point and scurried to the back of the warehouse, darting from shadow to shadow like a two-legged, blond rat. Then, outside, safe and sound, he released the breath.

Time's a-wastin', he warned himself. *Get on down to the docks, quick!* He swallowed. *Because how are you gonna explain it if somebody wants to know what you're doin' with a scuttle full of hot coals?*

Eyes on the prize, Bobby headed straight for O'Keefe's latest project, a beautiful schooner, still resting in its construction supports on the dock. He'd seen O'Keefe work on his boats, plenty of times. The man took great pride in his work, as evidenced by the glint in his eyes as he sawed and sanded and polished. But that expression of self-confidence and satisfaction was nothing compared to the look on his face when he worked on *Freedom Sails*. It was that very look that conceived the idea.

Bobby boarded the boat in one neat leap, landing on two feet on its polished mahogany decking. Crouching, he ran through the hatch—and caught his boot heel on the top step.

Down, down the narrow ladder he went, elbows and knees, hips and shoulders thumping walls and rails until he came to a stop in a heaping twist of arms and legs that forced the air from his lungs and flung hot coals in all directions.

Startled, he lurched and blinked as the now-empty coal scuttle landed with a clatter and the hatch slammed shut behind him.

When he caught his breath, Bobby whimpered quietly, trying to assess his injuries. There didn't seem to be a place on him that didn't ache, and it was dark, so very dark down there in the belly of the boat.

You're bleeding, he told himself, *bleeding bad.* But with so little light, he couldn't see what was bleeding or exactly how badly it was bleeding. He knew this much: On the way down, he'd snagged his hand on something—a nail? a hook? —making it impossible to determine if the gluey-wet substance along his trousers leg had come from the gash in his thigh or the wound on his palm. Wincing, he finger-walked down the outer seam of his pants, inching ever-closer to the source of his most excruciating pain.

His thumb touched something sharp, something jagged-edged and moist. "It's a bone. Your bone!" he hollered, amazed at how quickly this tightly-sealed compartment had swallowed up his voice. Waves of nausea and lightheadedness washed over him at the picture of it, poking out through the meaty flesh of his thigh.

"Doggone that stupid Mick," he whispered through pain-clenched teeth, "his confounded steep ladder. The fall has made you wet your pants." At least, in a long-forgotten part of his once-innocent heart, he hoped that's what had happened, because the alternative was simply too frightening.

With his good palm, Bobby patted along the floor until his fingers landed with a quiet splat. "No," he said. "Too thick, too sticky. It can only be—"

Blood.

A huge, quickly-spreading pool of it, oozing from the giant tear in the tissue of his leg.

Breathing hard, his heartbeat doubled, and closing his eyes, Bobby surrendered to the total blackness of unconsciousness.

❧

J. J. poured himself a cup of strong black coffee, intent upon finishing Burt's prosthesis that night.

Placing his mug on the far corner of the workbench, he perched on a high-backed chair facing the window and picked up a hank of leather. Following the pattern he'd sketched, J. J. used brass brads to secure one end of the harness to the wooden arm. A snip here, a stitch there, and he'd be ready to line the inside with cushiony shearing wool. It would be a poor substitute for the real thing, but at least when Burt strapped the arm on, he'd be able to use it to hold things steady while his good hand measured and pounded and sawed.

He leaned back, propped his feet on the table, and used a sharp, short-bladed knife to bevel the edges of the leather. Bits of tanned hide fell into his lap and onto the floor. No matter, he'd sweep it up when he cleaned the wood shavings and sawdust from the cabin floor of his pride and joy, *Freedom Sails*.

Movement in the distance caught his attention, and he looked up from his work.

The sight stunned him so badly, he nearly cut off his thumb. J. J. threw down the leather and the knife, as his booted feet hit the floor running.

Freedom Sails was on fire!

He was down the stairs and out of the warehouse in no time, and he covered the distance between the yard and the dock in a moment.

"J. J.!" Thaddius yelled. "Where you goin' in such a rush?"

Without missing a step and with teeth clenched in dogged determination, he pointed toward the shore.

"Good heavens," the old man said, staring in disbelief. "Mary! Pass the word: Fire!"

She was drying her hands on a tea towel when she stepped up behind him and peered over his shoulder. "Oh, heavens," she said, gasping. And in the next breath, she was hustling down the street, towel and apron flapping as she went store to store, spreading the word.

In minutes, Currituck's menfolk bounded from every door and thundered toward the dock. "We need to form a bucket brigade!" Thaddius instructed. "Start there, at the water's edge. Now let's shake a leg!"

J. J. hadn't heard the order. But even if he had, his only destination would have been *Freedom Sails*. He was onboard in no time, squinting into the murky, choking smoke, trying to locate its source. Tying a neckerchief around his mouth and nose to act as a filter, he raced around the deck. He quickly saw the deck was intact, but smoke was belching from the hold. Why was the hatch closed? Wondering what might have started the fire, he threw back the hatch.

Immediately, he was engulfed in a thick cloud of lung-clogging, eye-stinging smoke. Instinct made him crook an arm over his face, because the moment fresh air breathed over the fire, the flames broadened, lengthened, leapt through the opening like a trapped tiger that sees but one chance for escape and takes it in a desperate, forceful bound for freedom.

Muttering under his breath, he drove both his hands through hair, impatience and frustration mounting as he waited for the bucket brigade. What was taking them so long? *How difficult could it be,* he demanded, *to form a line and hand buckets down it?*

He was pacing now, coughing as he recounted the many spare hours he'd put into the building of this boat, the money, the energy. The boat was more, so much more, than a hulking thing created of leftovers and cast-off materials. He'd put more love and care into the sinking of these nails and the polishing of these boards than into anything he'd built thus far. Because he had fine plans for *Freedom Sails*. Why, even her name had—

What was that? J. J. wondered, motionless, save the blinking of his eyes. A voice, a boy's voice; no, a man's.

Could there be someone down there, amid the angry flames and the strangling smoke?

There it was again, that soft, agonized groan.

He took a step closer to the rectangular hole in the deck, craned his ear, listened. Yes, someone was down there. "Who" and "why" never entered his head. *If he's moaning, he's alive,* he thought, bending over to grasp the hatch handle.

"J. J.," Thaddius bellowed, "are you mad? You can't go down there!"

He was deaf to everything but the faint cries coming from below. Without a thought for his own safety, J. J. plunged into the roiling, rising cloud and, temporarily blinded by the eye-burning haze, felt his way down, down, along the wooden handrail.

Everything in him shouted, *Turn around, get out!*

He hesitated for a fraction of a second, considered heeding the warning; a week ago, he would have ignored it completely, wouldn't have given a second thought to diving into the inferno.

But a week ago, he didn't have much reason to love life. A week ago, he didn't know that Kate loved him.

"O'Keefe! Wait for the water line. Don't do it, man!"

But an undulating, tormented wail pierced the ebbing, flowing fumes, propelled him from his moment of indecision and prompted him onward.

It was as if the smoke was metamorphosing into a wheezing entity with a life of its own, churning, gurgling, gluttonously gobbling the air. How much longer could whoever was down there breathe? J. J. wondered, easing his way down the steep steps.

It was next to impossible to see in through the thick, smothering vapors, but he could make out a body sprawled just to the left of the ladder.

"Bobby?"

Immediately, he knew what had happened, and tension seized him, stiffening his limbs as if rigor mortis had set in. Bobby Banks had started the fire. He didn't know how and he didn't know why, but he was certain that the boy was responsible for it. *And knowin' Bobby, 'tweren't no accident.*

He could see that the boy was hurt, hurt badly. Could he continue holding his breath long enough to reach Bobby? And if he could, would he have the staying power to lift and carry him topside, to safety?

What had been a keening cry grew weaker, much weaker. There was no time for questions, even those of a life-saving kind.

Ye have to save him. At least, ye have to try.

And so he immersed himself into the thick of it, eyes narrowed and half-blinded by the prickling effects of the smoke. Down on one knee, he shoved one arm under Bobby's neck, the other under his knees. There was blood on the floor, dampening the knee of his trousers, slicking his knuckles and the backs of his hands, but he couldn't afford to waste one precious second determining its specific source. It was coming from Bobby. It was all J. J. needed to know to inspire him onward.

When J. J. started to lift, the boy loosed an agonizing, gut-wrenching scream that cut through him like a dagger. But he couldn't let it stop him. Whatever pain Bobby suffered now would be far more tolerable than the alternative.

Something was wrong with the boy's left arm, something dreadfully wrong, for it hung limp and useless at his side. But his right arm seemed fine, and he used it to cling to J. J. like a frightened babe.

J. J. knew he shouldn't open his mouth, shouldn't waste precious oxygen trying to speak. But an overwhelming sense that Bobby needed reassurance engulfed him. Whether the boy had set fire to the Norrises' house, whether he threatened to do the same to Kate and Adam, whether he'd come aboard this boat to carry out some form of devious destruction never crossed J. J.'s mind. Bobby was a boy, afraid and in horrific pain, and he couldn't help himself. "Easy, lad," he said, "take it easy.

Ye're gonna be fine." It was all he could manage before the smoke choked off the rest of what he wanted to say. But it seemed to have been enough to relax Bobby a bit.

J. J. stood, and when he shuffled his feet for better balance, his boot clanged into something metal. He caught a glimpse of it from the corner of his eye. *What's me coal scuttle doin' here?* he wondered. And it was his. He knew because he recognized the dent in its rim, the chip in its blue ceramic handle.

But the question of why or how it had gotten from the warehouse to the boat died as Bobby went limp in his arms. *Get him out of here! Get him into the fresh air.*

Turning sideways, to clear the hatch with his heavy load, J. J. willed himself to put one foot in front of the other.

Topside, the bucket brigade waited, and the man nearest the hatch—J. J. couldn't see who for the soot in his eyes— grabbed him by the scruff of the neck and helped pull him out. On the deck now, he steadied his footing and headed away, away from the fire and the smoke.

He trudged a distance of a hundred or so yards before his knees buckled. He sank slowly to the dock boards, cradling Bobby in his arms, and leaned, weak and spent and panting against a piling.

He had heard the clock tower in the village square counting the hours as he raced from the warehouse to the fire—eight peals to tell Currituckers the time. It was two minutes past eight now.

The fire fighters went about the business of getting the blaze under control as a crowd gathered 'round J. J. and Bobby. "Well, looky there. It's Bobby Banks," said a deep voice, "burnt and battered and bleedin'."

Another man said, "So there's justice in this old world after."

"Somebody get his da," J. J. growled. "Get the doc, too. The lad's in a bad way."

"Pa?" Bobby gasped. "Sorry, Pa."

"Hush, lad," J. J. instructed, a gentle hand of restraint on his shoulder.

"Never meant for 'em to die, Pa."

"Quiet, now," J. J. said, forcing a sternness into his voice that he did not feel. "Ye need to save yer strength."

"Just wanted—just wanted to scare 'em, that's all."

"He's rambling," said a woman.

"That's 'cause he's delirious," said another.

Bobby tried to sit up, but the pain knocked him flat again. "Coal," he whispered hoarsely. "Not. Wood chips an' sawdust ever'where, an'—"

J. J.'s gaze traveled the length of the boy, from sweat-dampened blond hair to blue eyes wild with agony to the gaping bloody wound in his thigh. He'd seen exposed muscle and bone before, and yet the sight set his stomach to rumbling and roiling.

He focused on Bobby's face, where tear-tracks washed clean swaths through the soot. His heart ached when he looked into those clear blue eyes, because though they were wide open and staring, they saw nothing. Nothing. It hit J. J. hard, like a solid fist to the jaw.

"Where's Peterson!" he demanded. "The lad's got two lungs full of smoke and he's bleedin' like a stuck pig. He needs tendin', and he needs it now!"

Bobby grew still, save the tremors that shook him head to heels. He met J. J.'s eyes, blinked once, twice, as if even that was a great effort. "You–you saved me," he rasped.

"Ye don't take well to instruction, do ye, lad?" J. J. said, his voice quaking. "I told ye to hush, save yer strength. Doc Peterson is on his way, and. . ."

Bobby's brow furrowed. "But why'd you save me?"

He brushed a lock of hair from Bobby's eyes. There was but one answer: "Had to."

He gave one slow nod of his head, and locked on J. J.'s gaze.

A sob ached in J. J.'s throat as he watched the light in his eyes dim, as he watched this young life slipping, ebbing, floating away. "Hold on, lad," he grated, giving his shoulders a shake. "Don't give up the ghost just yet. Fight, fight!"

J. J. shuddered. Would those evil things have damned him, without having lived long enough to experience regret or redemption?

But Bobby would not get that chance, and J. J. knew it.

He hung his head. "God's mercy on ye, lad; I'll say a prayer for yer immortal soul."

eight

They buried Bobby two days after the fire, with no one in attendance but Pastor Hall, Kate and J. J., and the boy's parents. His tombstone stood stock-straight, marking his final resting place with stone-cold granite. To the right, a stone read, *Beloved Brother.* To the left, one that read, *She will be missed.* Carved into Bobby's headstone, *Robert Lee Banks, Born December 15, 1841, Died July 15, 1855,* nothing more.

Amos Banks stepped away from the plot, weaving and bobbing as he grabbed for J. J.'s hand. "I heard what you tried to do for my boy."

Kate watched J. J.'s lips tighten, his brow furrow. "I'm sorry for your loss," was his craggy response.

The muscles in Amos's jaw bulged. "Risked your own skin to save him. Thank you."

Mrs. Banks sobbed.

J. J. said nothing.

"You probably think my boy was bad. No need to deny it, we both know it's true. And maybe he was, but then—" He ground his molars together. "That's right, it's whiskey you smell on my breath." He slid a flask from his pocket as if to prove it, and tilted it to his lips. "Weren't his fault, least-ways, not entirely. I rode him hard, was al'ays on him, never let up for a minute. Turned him mean, even meaner 'n me, I reckon." He paused, took another swig of the brew. "Wouldn't blame you if you judged me harsh."

"Ain't for me to judge ye, Banks," J. J. said quietly. "That's 'tween ye and yer Maker."

Never in her wildest dreams would she have thought she had anything in common with the likes of Amos Banks. But just days ago, Kate had spoken those very words to J. J. *How alike we all are after all,* she thought as the mourners drifted away.

She held her hand out to J. J.. "How about if I warm you a bit of that soup you made the other day?"

Smiling sadly, he took it, and together they walked away from the cemetery.

"You look tired, J. J. Maybe you'd rather just go home, get some much-needed sleep."

"Can't," he admitted. "I've tried." And in a lighter tone, "If I slept, I'd only dream of ye anyway; I'd much rather be with the real thing."

She put herself in front of him; he'd either have to stop, or tramp right over her.

He stopped.

Kate wiggled her forefinger, signaling him close. "Come here, Mr. O'Keefe."

And when he leaned down, she pressed a lingering kiss to his lips.

"What was that for?" he asked, grinning a bit.

"For being John Joseph O'Keefe, that's what."

She resumed walking. "I was about to tell you something the other day, when Adam came to. No, don't stop me," she instructed gently, "I'm afraid if I don't say it right out, I'll never say it at all."

Kate took a deep breath. Cleared her throat. "I know what folks must be saying, what they're probably thinking, what with the way we were, um, entangled on the Fourth of July.

"I've always been a proper lady, following God's rules and man's laws to the letter. To tell you the truth, I don't know if what I'm about to say is a violation of either."

"I doubt it," he interrupted. "Ye're as pure as new-fallen snow. Anything in yer head has got to be fine with the Almighty."

"I hope so. I truly hope so."

She'd been thinking about this for weeks, since before he'd kissed her on the Fourth, to be truthful. From the first story she'd heard about him, Kate had decided to keep a safe and careful distance from this man with the violent past. *Get too close,* she'd warned herself, *and you're liable to be the one he pummels and not for money, either!*

It hadn't taken long to learn that John Joseph O'Keefe had the gentlest soul, the sweetest temperament, the kindest disposition of any man she'd ever known, including her dear departed father! She discovered he was a practical man, realistic to the bone and logical to the end. He'd seen the advantages in his size and power, realized he could put it to good use, satisfying men's lust for blood and gore, because what else would they have let an Irish immigrant do to earn enough to buy and build a business!

The moment he was able, he'd set aside his gloves and stepped out of the ring, with no intention of returning. Amos Banks had goaded him into one last fight, but it had been his last fight. Thaddius had told her that J. J. swore he'd rather die of a beating than repeat a scene like that.

And then he'd stomped into her life, all bluster and blow, demanding retribution for a stolen lunch and the bucket he'd packed it in. She'd thought him petty and cheap at the time, scaring the wits out of her boy to reclaim a few pennies and a beat-up pail. Thought him a heathen, too. It hadn't taken long to figure out that it was because of his steadfast faith in God that his motives had been pure and true.

Adam had been a joy to be around since J. J. had come into their lives. Indeed, Adam wouldn't be alive if J. J. hadn't come into their lives!

He'd built *Freedom Sails* to help the people of Currituck. She could plainly see that he needed nothing more than a few creature comforts to keep him happy; the boat hadn't been constructed to add to his coffers.

Rather, it would carry the products and produce of the

town's hard-working citizens to ports north, where he'd sell the goods on their behalf and return with a tidy profit that Currituck's residents could build back into their businesses. Always the shrewd businessman and ever the poet, he believed the beauty of this small seacoast village might attract tourists one day.

"They'd come in droves," he'd teased, "and build houses right on the beach, so's they could get an eyeful of all the beauty the sea holds."

"A house on the beach!" she'd said, laughing. "What sort of fool would build a house on a foundation of sand!"

And he'd sighed. "You're right, of course." And smiled.

" 'Twould be quite a view, though. Meantime, *Freedom Sails* can be Currituck's conduit to security."

But first he had several weeks' worth of repairs to make because of fire and smoke damage to make *Freedom Sails* seaworthy.

"Will you show me the boat, J. J.?"

He halted. "But I thought. Ye said ye had somethin' to say."

"I can say it on the boat as easily as I can say it here. I've always wanted to see it; this way, we can kill two birds with one stone."

He slid his arms around her and pulled her close. "Kate, m' darlin', ye're a constant source of joy in me miserable life, d'ye know that?"

"And you in mine. Now," she said, pulling away, "last one there is a rotten egg!"

She hiked up her skirts and ran fast as her legs would carry her, feeling young and impetuous and free for the first time in nearly ten years, feeling womanly and wanted and loved for the first time in her life.

He could have caught up to her in three strides, she knew, what with those long, strong legs of his. Smiling, she thought, *how like him to let me win.*

Kate bounded up the plank that connected the dock to the

boat's deck and leaned her back against the rail. "Thank you," she said, breathless.

He took her in his arms. "For what?"

"Oh, nothing." She shrugged. "For being you, I guess."

"So, would ye like a tour?"

"I would."

She put her hand in his and let him tell her all the proper names of things, the stern, the bow, and bowsprit, the beam. "It's beautiful," she said when he was finished. "You're a true artist, J. J."

"Take hold of this," he said, handing her a rope.

"What is it?"

"It's the main halyard. I want ye to fasten it to the cleat, here," he explained, pointing to the squat iron T on the rail.

"But J. J.," she protested, giggling, "I don't know the first thing about—"

"Then it's high time ye learned, isn't it?" Guiding her hands, he taught her to "make fast," looping the rope around, then over and right, crossing under and left, and finishing with a snug loop.

"I give up, what'd we do that for?"

"I've been givin' it a lot of thought these past few days, Kate." J. J. nodded at the half-hitch.

"Why, it's almost exactly the way I tie a knot in my sewing!"

"Makes sense to me. It's strong and sure and trustworthy."

He wrapped his arms around her. "And so are you."

She batted her eyes flirtatiously. "J. J., stop. You'll give me a swelled head, comparing me to the likes of a knotted rope."

Chuckling, he held her near. " 'Twasn't meant as a physical comparison, m'darlin, 'cause Lord knows ye're far shapelier than a length of hemp." Hands on her shoulders, he held her at arm's length. "Ye're everything a woman ought to be, Kate Flynn. And in me humble opinion, there's but one thing wrong with ye."

She pouted prettily. "One thing? What thing?"

"Well. . .uh. . .it's yer—" He took a breath. "I. . .ah. . .we—"

"Yes?" she coaxed playfully.

"Well, how'd ye like yer people to be buried with me people?"

Her eyes widened. "What!"

"Well, they say an Irishman is too shy to ask outright what I'm tryin' to ask ye."

"Yes." She smiled prettily.

"All right, then," he said, "try this on for size: Kate O'Keefe." He grinned. "Now, doesn't that have a fine ring to it!"

Grinning playfully, she said, "If it came with a fine gold ring, it might."

Clasping her hands between his own, he looked toward the sky, exhaling a great huff of air as he closed his eyes. "Praise God Almighty!" And then he drove both fists heavenward in a gesture of joy and victory. "Thank God!" he bellowed.

He took a deep and calming breath before meeting her eyes. "I have a little somethin' for ye," he said, heading for the cockpit.

"A present? For me?" She felt like clapping her hands, like jumping up and down with glee, as a small girl might do on Christmas morning. "But why? It isn't my birthday or—"

"It's the first day of the rest of our lives," he said, uncovering a waist-high wooden crate. He grabbed a crowbar and pried off its lid, lifted a strange machine from inside.

"For me? Oh, J. J., how sweet." She pressed a knuckle against her teeth. "I'm sorry to be so dense, but what is it?"

"Why, it's a sewin' machine, of course. Brand new and right out of the foundry."

"A sewing machine?" Kate walked a wide circle around it to get a better look, smoothing her hands over its graceful curves, the slick-black enamel, the sleek oak drawers, the heavy iron legs. "How does it work?"

"Near as I can figure, you put the string up here."

"The thread," she corrected, winking.

He rolled his eyes. "You put the thread up here, weave it through this loop and that little arm, there, then through the eye of the needle. And when you tromp on the pedal, here, the needle goes up and down, and—" he spread his arms wide, "and ye're sewin'!"

She clasped her hands under her chin. "My! Whoever would have thought."

"Way I see it," he continued, hugging her from behind, "ye're gonna need all the time-savin' devices money can buy."

She leaned her head against his chest. "But why?"

"So ye'll have plenty of time for—"

Kate turned, rested both palms on his chest. "Are you talking about children, J. J.?"

His face ruddied with the beginnings of a blush, and he nodded.

"How many?"

"Many as ye'll give me," he said, smiling. Then, wiggling his eyebrows suggestively, he added, "but not so many that ye won't have time for me."

"Will you take me with you? When you bring the towns-folks' goods to Philadelphia and New York, I mean?"

"Wouldn't think of leavin' without ye!"

She threw her arms around his neck, then took a step back, frowning.

He gave her a worried look. "What? Ye haven't changed yer mind, have ye?"

"You're about to lose a button," she said, tapping his collar. "Good thing I'm a bit forgetful."

"Forgetful?"

She withdrew the needle she'd poked into her sleeve. "I keep it there when I'm working, so it'll always be within reach." Shrugging, she grinned. "Guess I forgot to take it out when I left." She grabbed his collar, stuck the fingers of her left hand inside it. "Now stand still, so I won't stick you."

In moments, the button was fastened, tight and sure. She wound the thread around it a few times. "What did you call it? A half-hitch?"

J. J. nodded.

"Well, there you have it, then. A button secured with a half-hitch."

Suddenly, she narrowed her eyes and, grinning, grabbed hold of his shirt. "But don't you get any fancy ideas," she warned teasingly.

"Ideas?"

"When you say 'I do' at our wedding, you'll be all the way hitched, got it?"

J. J. threw back his head and laughed. "Got it," he said.

Her smile softened, as did her voice. "Remember the Fourth of July, when you kissed me under the pines?"

"Only every other minute or so."

"When we were making that silly promise to call each other by our first names?"

"Ah, Missus soon-to-be O'Keefe, I love the way yer mind works. Ye wouldn't be suggestin' we seal this deal with a kiss, now would ye?"

"I insist on it."

When he came up for air, she combed her fingers through his beard. "Nice?" she asked with a tilt of her head.

"Very," he answered, feigning breathlessness.

"Well, that's just a sample of what you'll get once we've tied the knot for real."

A Letter To Our Readers

Dear Reader:

In order that we might better contribute to your reading enjoyment, we would appreciate your taking a few minutes to respond to the following questions. When completed, please return to the following:

Rebecca Germany, Managing Editor
Heartsong Presents
P.O. Box 719
Uhrichsville, Ohio 44683

1. Did you enjoy reading *Kate Ties the Knot?*
   ❑ Very much. I would like to see more books
     by this author!
   ❑ Moderately
     I would have enjoyed it more if _____

     _____

2. Are you a member of **Heartsong Presents**? ❑Yes ❑No
   If no, where did you purchase this book?_____

   _____

3. What influenced your decision to purchase this book? (Check those that apply.)

   ❑ Cover   ❑ Back cover copy

   ❑ Title   ❑ Friends

   ❑ Publicity   ❑ Other_____

4. How would you rate, on a scale from 1 (poor) to 5 (superior), the cover design?_____

5. On a scale from 1 (poor) to 10 (superior), please rate the following elements.

      __Heroine   __Plot

      __Hero   __Inspirational theme

      __Setting   __Secondary characters

6. What settings would you like to see covered in **Heartsong Presents** books?_____

_____

_____

7. What are some inspirational themes you would like to see treated in future books?_____

_____

_____

8. Would you be interested in reading other **Heartsong Presents** titles? ❑ Yes ❑ No

9. Please check your age range:
   ❑ Under 18   ❑ 18-24   ❑ 25-34
   ❑ 35-45   ❑ 46-55   ❑ Over 55

10. How many hours per week do you read? _____

Name _____

Occupation _____

Address _____

City_____State_____Zip _____

An Old-Fashioned Christmas

Four new inspirational love stories
from Christmases gone by

God Jul by Tracie Peterson

Sigrid may be resigned to spinsterhood, but she is not ready to sell the family homestead. Two men have approached her about marriage. In whose ear will Sigrid whisper "God Jul" (Merry Christmas)?

Chrsitmas Flower by Colleen L. Reece

Shana cannot ignore the feeling that God is leading her away from her beloved Alaska. But what about her childhood friend, Wyatt, who insists on following her all the way to North Carolina?

For the Love of a Child by Sally Laity

This Christmas, can two lonely adults be drawn togher by the plaintive cry of a child in the cold Philadelphia night?

Miracle on Kismet Hill by Loree Lough

High on Kismet Hill, Brynne surveys the magnificent vista below and wonders about her future, ravaged by the Civil War. One man she loved could be dead, one man she loved betrayed her, and the third. . . She simply can't risk being wrong again.

(352 pages, Paperbound, 5" x 8")

Send to: Heartsong Presents Reader's Service
             P.O. Box 719
             Uhrichsville, Ohio 44683

Please send me _____ copies of *An Old-Fashioned Christmas*.
I am enclosing **$4.97 each** (please add $1.00 to cover postage
and handling per order. OH add 6.25% tax. NJ add 6% tax.).
Send check or money order, no cash or C.O.D.s, please.
   To place a credit card order, call 1-800-847-8270.

NAME _____

ADDRESS _____

CITY/STATE _____ ZIP _____

······Hearts♥ng ·······

Any 12 *Heartsong Presents* titles for only **$26.95** *

*plus $1.00 shipping and handling per order and sales tax where applicable.

HISTORICAL ROMANCE IS CHEAPER BY THE DOZEN!

Buy any assortment of twelve *Heartsong Presents* titles and save 25% off of the already discounted price of $2.95 each!

HEARTSONG PRESENTS TITLES AVAILABLE NOW:

___HP 64   CROWS'-NESTS AND MIRRORS, *Colleen L. Reece*

___HP103   LOVE'S SHINING HOPE, *JoAnn A. Grote*

___HP111   A KINGDOM DIVIDED, *Tracie J. Peterson*

___HP112   CAPTIVES OF THE CANYON, *Colleen L. Reece*

___HP131   LOVE IN THE PRAIRIE WILDS, *Robin Chandler*

___HP132   LOST CREEK MISSION, *Cheryl Tenbrook*

___HP135   SIGN OF THE SPIRIT, *Kay Cornelius*

___HP140   ANGEL'S CAUSE, *Tracie J. Peterson*

___HP143   MORNING MOUNTAIN, *Peggy Darty*

___HP144   FLOWER OF THE WEST, *Colleen L. Reece*

___HP163   DREAMS OF GLORY, *Linda Herring*

___HP167   PRISCILLA HIRES A HUSBAND, *Loree Lough*

___HP168   LOVE SHALL COME AGAIN, *Birdie L. Etchison*

___HP175   JAMES'S JOY, *Cara McCormack*

___HP176   WHERE THERE IS HOPE, *Carolyn R. Scheidies*

___HP179   HER FATHER'S LOVE, *Nancy Lavo*

___HP180   FRIEND OF A FRIEND, *Jill Richardson*

___HP183   A NEW LOVE, *VeraLee Wiggins*

___HP184   THE HOPE THAT SINGS, *JoAnn A. Grote*

___HP187   FLOWER OF ALASKA, *Colleen L. Reece*

___HP188   AN UNCERTAIN HEART, *Andrea Boeshaar*

___HP191   SMALL BLESSINGS, *DeWanna Pace*

___HP192   FROM ASHES TO GLORY, *Bonnie L. Crank*

___HP195   COME AWAY MY LOVE, *Tracie J. Peterson*

___HP196   DREAMS FULFILLED, *Linda Herring*

___HP199   DAKOTA DECEMBER, *Lauraine Snelling*

___HP200   IF ONLY, *Tracie J. Peterson*

___HP203   AMPLE PORTIONS, *Dianne L. Christner*

___HP204   MEGAN'S CHOICE, *Rosey Dow*

___HP207   THE EAGLE AND THE LAMB, *Darlene Mindrup*

___HP208   LOVE'S TENDER PATH, *Birdie L. Etchison*

(If ordering from this page, please remember to include it with the order form.)

·········· Presents ··········

Great Inspirational Romance at a Great Price!

Heartsong Presents books are inspirational romances in contemporary and historical settings, designed to give you an enjoyable, spirit-lifting reading experience. You can choose wonderfully written titles from some of today's best authors like Peggy Darty, Sally Laity, Tracie Peterson, Colleen L. Reece, Lauraine Snelling, and many others.

*When ordering quantities less than twelve, above titles are $2.95 each.
Not all titles may be available at time of order.*

SEND TO: Heartsong Presents Reader's Service
        P.O. Box 719, Uhrichsville, Ohio 44683

Please send me the items checked above. I am enclosing $_____.
(please add $1.00 to cover postage per order. OH add 6.25% tax. NJ add
6%). Send check or money order, no cash or C.O.D.s, please.
        To place a credit card order, call 1-800-847-8270.

NAME _____

ADDRESS _____

CITY/STATE _____ ZIP _____

HPS 13-97

Heartsong Presents
Love Stories Are Rated G!

That's for godly, gratifying, and of course, great! If you love a thrilling love story, but don't appreciate the sordidness of some popular paperback romances, **Heartsong Presents** is for you. In fact, **Heartsong Presents** is the *only inspirational romance book club*, the only one featuring love stories where Christian faith is the primary ingredient in a marriage relationship.

Sign up today to receive your first set of four, never before published Christian romances. Send no money now; you will receive a bill with the first shipment. You may cancel at any time without obligation, and if you aren't completely satisfied with any selection, you may return the books for an immediate refund!

Imagine. . .four new romances every four weeks—two historical, two contemporary—with men and women like you who long to meet the one God has chosen as the love of their lives. . .all for the low price of $9.97 postpaid.

To join, simply complete the coupon below and mail to the address provided. **Heartsong Presents** romances are rated G for another reason: They'll arrive *Godspeed!*

YES! Sign me up for Heartsong!

NEW MEMBERSHIPS WILL BE SHIPPED IMMEDIATELY!
Send no money now. We'll bill you only $9.97 post-paid with your first shipment of four books. Or for faster action, call toll free 1-800-847-8270.

NAME _____

ADDRESS _____

CITY _____ STATE _____ ZIP _____

MAIL TO: HEARTSONG PRESENTS, P.O. Box 719, Uhrichsville, Ohio 44683

YES10-96